YOUTH
IN THE WIND

A NOVEL OF HOPE AND COURAGE

The human being is neither an angel nor a beast.
The great misfortune is the one who appears to be an angel
But is really a beast.

MARIA TZIMAS

YOUTH IN THE WIND

Quantity sales special discounts are available on quantity purchases by corporations, associations, and others. For details, contact the publisher at the address above.

Orders by U.S. trade bookstores and wholesalers. Email info@BeyondPublishing.net

Th e Beyond Publishing Speakers Bureau can bring authors to your live event. For more information or to book an event contact the Beyond Publishing Speakers Bureau speak@BeyondPublishing.net

Th e Author can be reached directly at BeyondPublishing.net

Manufactured and printed in the United States of America distributed globally by BeyondPublishing.net

BEYOND
PUBLISHING

New York | Los Angeles | London | Sydney

Library of Congress Control Number: 2022900181

ISBN Hardcover: 978-1-637922-50-7

CHILDREN are like flowers.

Both are beautiful, but lack strength.

Flowers die once, but children are maltreated every day.

The child, since the creation of the world, has been the victim of all the sadists and perverts, such Herod and Hitler, and so many others, who are daily responsible for numerous childhood tragedies. Then, we shall see how the child has been victimized.

Many organizations have been formed to protect the children, but looking about us, it seems ironic that they are not able to do very much.

Pain does not have color, but it has a face, and we see that face daily, in millions of pale and skinny faces.

Personally, I never was a child.

I never played with toys.

I never held a doll.

I lived a sad and melancholy childhood, and I know its "cost".

Youth in the Wind is a story that will touch everyone's heart, and will give hope to a younger generation.

Maria Tzimas

TABLE OF CONTENTS

IN A BAR

I didn't know the man. I had never ever heard his name. If I had read of his murder in the papers, I wouldn't have given it a second thought. Besides, a seaman like me rarely reads papers. I say 'like me' because I'm not very sociable and not at all conventional. I am—or rather, I was—a carefree chap. I have no liking for papers. It's wrong of me, of course, but that's how I'm made, rather headstrong, and I like to have my own way.

I always disliked papers. They made my head swim.....Besides, I always managed to find out what was happening in the world. I got to hear of things in my various ports of call, briefly and in a general sort of way, I was given the news by people who are ever eager to import information.

That morning, however, the barman of the joint where I had been making myself at home for the last two days, handed me a paper, saying, "Here, Greek, read this bit of news. It might interest you."

The only bit of news that could have interested in me at that moment was where I could find Terezina. But at the sight of his worried look, I cast an indifferent glance at the part of the paper he was pointing to. My indifference immediately turned to terror, anguish, panic, and such unbearable pain that if the barman hadn't held me up, I would have crumpled to the floor in a dead faint. Not because of the man who had been found dead in a brothel with six bullets in his body. His name was Tom Kronov, but as I have told you, I didn't know the fellow.

He had, however, been murdered by Terezina, my wife of twenty-four hours..... But that was only the beginning. And I, all unawares, having absolutely no connection with the man, was involved in this tragic story...

My name is John Moschakis. I'm a seaman. By the way, what's your opinion of seamen? And especially of a twenty-six-year-old seaman who marries a prostitute? No doubt, you'll say he's a fool. Right. I say 'right' because that is the general opinion. But if I had married a rich girl? Then everyone would have said: "Well done". Right again, that's the general opinion. But is general opinion always right?

Now, in order to go into the meaning of general opinion, I need time and paper, plenty of both, and as I don't give a bugger for other people's opinions and have adopted the first rule of the hippies: "Disregard other people's opinion;" I married an eighteen-year-old prostitute.

When I proposed marriage to her, she looked daggers at me. I remember that look so well and I wonder why I wasn't struck dead on the spot by such a glance.

I am an ordinary fellow. Not of the lowest social order, but certainly not of the middle class. I have no connection whatsoever with high society. So, I can readily send all those high and mighty rich to the devil, all those gilded aristocrats who believe that human lives and human dignity can be bought.

I even send to the devil all who claim to preach the truth, for them a non-existent truth. Unfortunately, they are steeped in lies. That's my personal opinion, which is not groundless..... I don't like to drink. Although I've been a sailor since I was fifteen years old, and have travelled all over the world in leaky old wrecks or in luxury liners, I have always kept to soft drinks.

Soft drinks of the worst quality, on the deck of a ship or on the sidewalk of a seaport...

My mother tried to bring up her children decently. Of course, I wasn't a namby-pamby, nor did I follow the family tradition to the letter; I was a bit of lad. But I have one good point, some might call it a failing: I'm as stubborn as a mule. However, I have always kept a tight hand on my purse-strings, and I have always tried to increase my hoard, because between you and me, you can put up with the sea as long as you are young and strong. But when your back begins to bend and your face and hands start to wrinkle—in other words, when you show signs of cracking up, as we seamen say—you'll be sent to rot in any old port, along with the leaky wrecks that are left to molder in the sun...

As a prudent seaman, I have decided to be the first to break up the partnership with the sea. So, I saved up like mad, avoiding any unnecessary expense, such as standing rounds of drinks to colleagues.

I had never set foot in a bar. What a disgrace for a twenty-six-year-old seaman: eleven years at sea should have turned me into a confirmed drunkard. But it was not so. To this day, I don't know what made me go into that bar that night, rubbing my hands to get them warm, stamping my feet and shaking the snow off my shoulders. Was it the cold that compelled me to enter the bar? Or was it my loneliness? I daresay it was the cold, because I was trembling all over, in spite of my warm duffle coat, my woolen sweater, and my thick trousers.

It is devilishly cold in New York, especially round about Christmas. The cold freezes your blood and pierces you to the bone. And it was Christmastime then. I'll never forget that Christmas, even if I live to be a hundred.

At first, I had difficulty getting used to the dim light; I would never have imagined that it would have been so dark and so quiet in a bar on Broadway, in the very heart of New York...

I don't know whose idea the lighting was. But I must admit that I liked it. It was pleasant in there. I climbed onto one of the high stools that were lined up, then I looked round me, casting slanting glances here and there are bestowing smiles on two gentlemen as I rather awkwardly squeezed in between them. My eyes fell on the color T.V., which at that moment was showing the latest trip of the astronauts to the Moon. All had their eyes fixed on the screen. Eyes full of admiration and wonder...

But I was not magnetized by the T.V. I won't say that I was not moved by the superhuman achievements of science, but the fact is that I have a roving eye, so my glance wandered searchingly round the bar, and suddenly, it came to rest on two superb female legs. They belonged to a young girl who was sitting at the opposite table.

My glance gradually began to creep upwards; I saw an evening dress that stressed the curves of her body that had the perfect proportions of a classical statue. Then, I saw two bright red lips, two blue eyes, and hair like twenty-four carat spun gold.

She was not just beautiful. She was ethereal. She was the type of woman that men gaze at like idiots. A fascinating woman. Her every movement was a silent challenge to the wildest, basest instincts of man. There was a strange contrast in her. Her body was that of a woman created for lust. Her face was that of an innocent, immaculate virgin. Her hair had been styled by a master hairdresser. Her beauty was of a kind that is not flattered by the camera. It was so perfect, so unbelievable. I tried to get my thoughts under control. I opened and shut my eyes, thinking that perhaps, the faint light of the bar was playing a nasty trick on me. But when I opened my eyes again, the fairylike creature was still there, now holding a glass of amber-colored drink between her tapering fingers, tipped with bright red nails.

Her lips moved. But the sound she shuttered was not melodious as I had expected. It was a voice that would make a musician take flight like a hunted hare, or that would reduce a child to screams of terror. It was slightly hoarse, both rasping and wheezy, like a wretched old locomotive struggling uphill.

"Fix me another drink, boy," said the voice.

"What, another one!" exclaimed the boy. The boy was the barman, a man of sixty, with a tired, kindly face and pure white hair. You could guess that he cared for others more than he cared for himself.

"Don't I pay you?" hissed the voice, like a cobra ready to attack.

"Yes, you do," admitted the boy, rather at a loss.

"So, fill up my glass and stop talking a lot of blah and wasting calories. I don't want you to have a breakdown, Boy." That was the answer of my fairylike vision.

"You're drinking too much, and it's bad for you." advised the Boy.

"Thanks for the advice, but I've had enough for tonight, and as you are so mindful of your client's welfare, why don't you close down your lousy old bar?" she sneered. Crossing her beautiful legs and resting her cheek on her right hand, she waited for the barman's reply.

"Even if I do close down the bar, you'll find some other place to go to," he answered heatedly.

"Now that was very smart!" she said clapping her hands. "Since the day I first met you, it's the first time I've heard you say something smart…"

The barman shook his head melodramatically, like a bad actor, then he filled up her glass.

She took it between her hands, held it up to the light, uttered an exclamation and downed it, as if it were spring water. She wiped the drops from her lips with the back of her hand. She clicked her tongue with pleasure, and while I expected to see her drop to the floor, she held out her glass again saying, "Bullshit, we're not content with our life here on Earth, so we're going to try living on the Moon, fiddlesticks! Poppycock! Hey, Boy, same again."

Without saying a word, "Boy" filled her glass again. You could tell from his movements that she was driving him from desperation.

"You barmen are pitiful creatures. On the one hand, you want us to empty your bottles and fill your tills, and on the other hand, you dole out advice. You're not on the level. You're sly, two-faced devils. And you are the biggest devil of them all!"

"How did you guess that I am a devil?" he asked with the hint of a smile on his thick, cherry-red lips.

"I guessed it because I'm a little devil, too. Little but smart."

"And what makes you think you're smart?" the barman asked aggressively, crossing his arms on his chest.

She answered him with a question; "Has anybody told you that I'm dumb?"

"That has," said the barman, triumphantly pointing to her glass.

"You're wrong there, Boy. That doesn't mean I'm dumb; that means I'm clever. My father may have been a no-go drunkard, but he begot me, a cure and dainty soak."

"Will you let me tell you something?" he asked.

"Fire away, Boy. I like to hear you preaching. That's to say I like to hear you talking nonsense, like those sky pilots who never stop sermonizing. They never stop coming to your bar either, to wet their whistles that have gone dry from too much talking."

"I'm not a sky pilot, as you call the pastors," he said pointing to his white apron, "and I don't sermonize, nor do I wet my whistles with booze to keep it from rusting. I've seen others here before you, doing what you're doing now, and then suddenly, I saw them no more."

"Really?" What happened? Did they have a flat tire?" she asked, pretending surprise and playing with her empty glass.

"Well, not exactly, but if you want to put it that way, they were found flat out, and…"

"Flat out," she interrupted.

"Yes, flat, croaked, dead," he answered testily.

"What from? Was it from too many worries?"

"I told you, and I made it clear, not from too many worries, but from too much drink."

"Is that the sober truth?"

"Do you think I'm in the mood for sick jokes?"

"But that's wonderful," she cried, spinning round on her chair, "fill up my glass, quick."

He looked at her for a moment disapprovingly, then he passed her the bottle.

"Here you are, take it and drink till morning. I can't spend all my time talking to you. I've got other costumers to tend to."

She didn't seem to mind his angry tone, she just filled her glass and drained it in one long draught. Then, she re-filled it and called out to the barman: "Listen, Boy."

"What's up again?"

"All these people here, why do they drink?" and she pointed to the customers of the bar. "Are they in the doldrums?"

"What was that you said?" he asked as he approached, puzzled at the word she had used.

"Don't tell me you've never heard that word before: 'doldrums', you stupid American! How can you be so dumb—it's not as if you were a crossbreed. Get lost now, go and see to your customers and fill your till. But even if you don't fill it, never you mind, I'll be here to make up for the loss."

"I see that kid is a regular soak," I said to the barman when he eventually came round to serve me.

"I'm sorry for her, that's all I can say. I'm terribly sorry for her, she downs so much booze every day, that's it's a wonder how her liver can stand it and hasn't burst yet. You'd think she'd been born a drinker, that she'd sucked up the stuff as a baby," said the barman.

"I'd say she was well-born, and she doesn't seem to be sparing with her money," I said somewhat cynically.

"I don't know what to say," answered the barman. "She may be of a good family, even an aristocratic family, that has come down in the world and she can't get used to it. Listen, young man, this world is a mysterious place. I can't make out some people who seem to have everything, like this little smasher. Yet, she comes here and sucks up whole bottles-full of booze, you'd think she was a sponge. But shall I tell you something? Maybe you won't believe it, but it's the truth. When she doesn't come, I get terribly worried. I like to see her here, but she's so elusive. All my customers like to see her here in the bar."

She had been listening, but she hadn't said a word. She just glanced at the barman, who was sulkily wiping his hands on a dirty cloth, then she glanced at me with curiosity. She filled her glass with a yellowish liquor, but before bringing it to her lips, she looked at it and asked, "Why doesn't he send me packing?"

The barman heard her and went near. "We've already spoken about that. If I send you away, you'll go somewhere else."

"So you're afraid of losing a customer, you old bastard."

"If you like to think so, okay,"

"Well, isn't is so? Can you tell me how many bucks I leave in your lousy old dive every day? Have you kept count, because I haven't taken the xxx trouble to. I take the dough out of my bag by the handful, and you grab it in your rotten mitts. How many bucks each time? I bet you've counted them many a time. How many? Fifty, a hundred? More or less? Show me another customer who leaves you more, and then send me away. As for my aristocratic origin, I'll tell you something and get it clear: if all aristocrats had the same aristocratic origin as me, they would have nothing to be proud of."

The barman didn't answer her. Besides, what could he say? He knew she was right. From what I gathered, she was speaking the truth. Yes. She threw the dollars by the handful onto his counter. She didn't ask how many there were; she didn't ask for change. I wondered why.

"Now I've hurt her. Yes, I've hurt her. I shouldn't have. I shouldn't have," muttered the old man regretfully.

"Don't use dirty words, you old sod. Don't be thankful to those who give without asking for anything in return," she said, with a hint of a sob in her voice.

The barman was just about to say something, but she took the bottle in her hand again and picked up a glass, giving him to understand that the matter should end there.

I sat listening, full of curiosity. I could hardly believe my ears or my eyes. The stool I was perched on was the nearest to her little table. So I could not help hearing every word of that strange and not very choice conversation. The other customers hadn't even turned around. Besides, their attention was on the astronauts. They had either not heard anything, or else they were so used to such scenes that they took them in their stride.

The two gentlemen who had been sitting on either side of me had left long ago. The TV program was still on. And I was still sitting on my stool, holding the brandy I had ordered and which I had not even tasted. I could not help feeling uneasy, and this uneasiness gradually dispelled my happy mood.

By nature, man is a strange creature. Very strange. My uneasiness stemmed from the disappointment this ethereal creature was causing me. So charming to look at. So beautiful. So terribly beautiful.

Then, I didn't know, but now, I can say what it was that made me take an interest in that girl. I'm not a coward. I had known lots and lots of women, and I had got the better of them all. But this one was something different. Quite unusual. I pondered a long time before getting off my stool, brandy in hand, and walking towards her table.

I stopped in front her, still undecided. Speechless. I just looked at her. I looked at her and tried to make out some sign of pain or despair on her little face. I saw none...

She fixed her glance on me, and then I saw from close up that her clear blue eyes were like two pieces of Attic sky.

"Scram!" she said. I didn't stir.

"I'm a Greek passing through," I said. "I heard that you are Greek, too, so I wondered if you would like us to have a chat about our distant homeland."

"Not so distant," she replied. "You can be there in eight hours, by plane, so hurry up and go there and have your chat, because I'm in no mood for talking."

I avoided answering her. "Your eyes remind me of the land where I was born and reared, and which I haven't seen for years," I said, this time assuming a sorrowful air.

"How many years?" she asked.

"Six," I answered dryly.

"Six," she repeated, "that's an unlucky number. Take a seat, but don't talk, just drink."

"I don't drink," I said curtly, "I only want a chat."

"I can't talk without drinking, my throat gets dry, and besides, I don't want to get dehydrated. That's what the boys in white say, isn't it?" There was a sneer in her voice. I guessed she was speaking about doctors.

"Alright, have it your way," she said. I made myself comfortable on a chair, and at last, I brought the brandy to my lips. She was watching me. At least five minutes passed like that.

Then, she began to drink again. "To your health, fellow-countryman, and to the health of all our folk."

I didn't speak. She had a drink, then another and another. "My feet have stopped hurting me after walking all the afternoon," she said, "and the dark thoughts have cleared from my mind, *swish, swish*, they've flown like frightened birds. I feel as though I were wrapped in a fluffy blanket. I feel happy."

"That's fine," I agreed. "Happiness is a rare thing."

"Don't talk nonsense, Greek," she scolded. "Happiness isn't a thing. Greeks shouldn't talk such nonsense. They'll lose the reputation they've got of being smart."

"You're right," I agreed again. "Happiness isn't a thing. The Greeks shouldn't talk nonsense, but they shouldn't despair either."

I let that drop, just to see what her reaction would be.

"Greek, shut up." Then, she looked at her glass and said, "That's why I love you, you bloody thing. You help me to forget. You chase away all my frightening thoughts… Do you know of any human being who can do that?"

I seized the opportunity, like a drowning man catches hold of a straw. "I," I said, pointing to myself and stretching myself to my full height. "Tell me what frightens you. Tell me who scares you, and I'll make short work for him. I'm not yellow, believe you me."

Suddenly, she stopped drinking and fixed her gaze on me so intently that I felt as if I had ceased to exist. There were only those blue eyes, two blue pools, and I realized that I was about to drown in those pools, whatever perils they might hide, whatever havoc they might make on me. For the first time in my life, I had the feelings that things were beyond my control. I was unable to utter a word, and my head felt as if it had been dealt a heavy blow. That moment was the moment of my life.

Her voice recalled me to reality.

"Greek, get lost. Get out of my sight. I'm the mermaid, the sister of Alexander the Great, and I give no quarter. I'll wreck the ship that brought you here, and of course, I'll do away with you, too."

"Fine," I said, recovering my voice. "For years, I've been searching for the legendary mermaid, and now here, I find her in a bar, swimming in whisky."

"You're stark, staring mad," she said, with such a sweet smile on her full, tempting lips that I don't know how I kept myself from snatching her into my arms.

I merely said, "Do you know of a seaman who's not mad? They'll all crazy, every one of them. It's the sea that drives them mad, my mermaid."

She pondered for a while and then suddenly, the expression on her face became so hard, so fierce that I was scared. Then, she rested her two hands on the table and half rose. She grabbed the bottle and lifted it, as if to throw it at my head.

"Scram," she roared like a lioness. "Scram, you bloody bastard."

I didn't move an inch. I just stretched out my hand and took the bottle away from her. Then, I banged it hard on the table and smashed it into pieces. Glass and booze scattered all over the place.

Everybody turned round to look at us, but only for a moment. They were used to such incidents for they soon turned their eyes towards the TV again.

The Greek girl was now sitting quietly on her chair, and I was introducing myself calmly, as if nothing had happened.

"My name is John....."

"That will do," she cut in, "that's enough. My name is Terezina. Terry for short, which will you have? They both go to the highest bidder."

"I like Terezina," I said. "Anyway, pleased to meet you."

"I think you'd better say 'sorry'," she answered.

"Why should I be sorry?"

"Because whoever gets to know me lives to regret it," she said, with a touch of bitterness on her voice.

"But I'm sure you'll bring me luck," I said.

"You're wrong there, John. Quite wrong."

"Have it your own way." I said. "I see you speak Greek very well."

"That's what is left of a not-quite-forgotten language, John," she replied. "You can't forget your mother-tongue in six short years, not even in six centuries. If you forget it, then you're a traitor to your country. A traitor to the mother who bore you and suffered in vain to bring you into the world."

Her words were like steel grip round my heart. I had to bring the brandy to my lips again to ease the feeling of oppression.

This young girl, who was acting hardboiled and rebellious was nothing but a frightened kid. Badly frightened and embittered, and I felt a newfound feeling urging me to sink or swim with her. My destiny, my very life were in her hands. I was now sure that all my life up to that day had been empty, and that I had been searching for her in my dreams.

Sometimes, I had felt ashamed, but that's how it was. I used to dream a lot. I was always having dreams. Children have vivid imaginations, and no one thinks it strange. They fancy themselves as hunters, airmen, fighters, skippers, astronauts, according to the current vogue.

But it's rather different when you're grown up, at least that's what people say. But you can't live without dreams. I bet I'm not the only man in the world who dreams—or, rather, who has daydreams—even at the age of twenty-six; some imagine they are rich, others that they are young, others that they'll do something important before they die.

So, now, with Terezina, I was no longer an insignificant seaman, sailing the seven seas in quest of fortune. Of course, I was poor, but with all due modesty, I can say that I was handsome and strong, qualities I would use to conquer this apparition I had met here in this dimly-lit bar.

But tell me, who is the man who knows exactly the time and place of his dreams? No one, absolutely no one. Moments mark our lives, not years, and I'll bet my sweet life on that.

While I was watching her, and all those thoughts were rushing through my mind, she went on drinking, as if she would never stop.

"Hey! Old bastard!" she called out.

I realized it was the liquor talking now, and that it was too late to intervene between Terezina and her drunkenness.

I felt that I was nothing but an insignificant seaman once more who had nothing better to do than drink in the company of a harbor whore. I shuddered. *No,* said a voice within me, *Terezina isn't a whore, she's just a little girl gone astray, but her soul is pure and untouched by corruption.*

"If you forget your mother-tongue, then you're a traitor to your country. A traitor to the mother who bore you." Were those the words of a whore? Would a prostitute speak like that to a sailor she'd just met casually in a bar?" Would a prostitute be so smartly and tastefully dressed? Would her beauty be so ethereal, so unbelievable? Impossible. Terezina was not a prostitute. She was…

She didn't even notice that I had moved away from her and was approaching the barman.

"This time I want a whisky," I said, "with ice. Make it strong, I need it badly."

Before he had time to serve me, I heard her voice again, hoarse and angry.

"Hey, old bastard! Come over here and bring me another bottle."

He turned to me almost in tears. "Did you hear that? I've never had such a case like that in my forty-year career as a barman."

He walked across the bar with heavy steps to take her the new bottle.

"Haven't you had enough yet? How much longer are you going on drinking?"

She lifted her hand and gave him a slap, which was more like a caress.

"You old bastard! Haven't I told you that I don't want any advice? Tonight, I must drink more than any other time. I must drink until I burst, like those people you were telling me about."

"I can't make you out this evening, I can't make you out." he muttered.

"I don't want you to make me out, you old sod, I asked you to bring me a bottle of whisky. I asked for more drink, which I pay you for; I'm not asking for charity, I hate charity just as you hate your black customers, those you despise when they come into your bar, as you despise me now. Be careful though, old sod, I don't give a bugger for your scorn. Mind you, don't get it in the neck one day from the blacks; be more decent with them, because between you, me, and the doorpost, we whites are worse blackguards than those poor blacks, whose only sin is the color of their skin. Never forget, old sod, that the worst disasters in the world have been brought about by the whites." She stopped and looked at him questioningly.

"Don't you agree, Boy?"

"I agree," he answered thoughtfully.

"So, you see, although I'm tipsy, I talk sense. And now, before we part, could you tell me the name of that bastard fellow-countryman of mine, that Greek, who first invented booze?"

"I'm afraid I can't."

"You are a fool, Boy! I never thought you were such a fool. Now bugger off, and no more of your advice."

"I feel pity for you, that's all I can say," he replied as he turned to serve me.

She laughed and shook her head as she filled up her glass from the new bottle....

"Who does the barman pity? Did you hear that? He pities me! I'm a queen, and yet, he pities me! The old bastard must be drunk to talk like that," she muttered to herself.

She got up, opened her bag, took some money out, and threw it onto the table without counting it. Her legs were not shaky. Her walk was steady, and she held her head high, as if the world belonged to her. Only the heels of her shoes seemed wobbly. Yes, the heels were to blame. Why did women wear high heels? God had sent them into the world barefoot.

"Why will men go against their God?" she murmured. "Why did they invent shoes?" She took off her shoes and threw them into the corner. As she got to the door, she stopped and turned to the barman, "Bye, Boy, see you tomorrow, first thing in the morning, when I come for breakfast... And look here, no grumbling. You and I are birds of a feather. You sell, I buy. So why should we break-up with partnership?"

He shook his head.

"To hell with me if I can make any sense out of that kid," he said to me, as soon as Terezina had gone through the door.

She may have heard him, but she didn't turn round. She went into the street, head held high. The sky was black. The street was white with snow, but she didn't seem to feel the cold. She stood barefoot in the snow at the edge of the sidewalk.

"Taxi, taxi," I heard her hail a cab.

I was just about to get up and follow her, but the barman stopped me.

"No," he said, "not tonight."

His words were an order. Firm and decisive. His hand gripped my arm hard, harder than necessary. I didn't follow her, and as I turned to look at him, I wondered at the anguish on his face.

"You mustn't follow her," he repeated. "Get this right, Greek, that girl's life is a mystery that has got me flummoxed. I know so little about her. Not much more than you do. But just listen to this. She is often fetched away from the bar by a lady of quality, an aristocrat I should say. She comes loaded with jewels and smothered in furs. She has told me to keep an eye on the girl. So, in here, no one dares make up to her.

So don't do anything foolish, Greek. You heard her say she'll be here in the morning. What do you say about putting our heads together, you and I? Shall we try to get to the bottom of mystery? Because I'm sure that a mystery surrounds her."

"I'd say okay, though it doesn't seem an easy task."

"Alright, I'll be here in the morning, so come, and we'll see what we can do to solve this riddle."

ANTICIPATION

Tomorrow seemed an age in coming. It often happens like that. The anticipation of joy or success is killing. The clock seems to stop, and its hands are like the legs of an overloaded donkey that refuses to budge.

As I lay on the couch in my third-rate hotel, my eyes fixed on the clock, my thoughts wandered to the convicts in the death-cell. How they would bless a clock for not moving its hands! When death is near, the hours pass quickly. But when you are waiting for life, the time drags on…

I don't know if I slept that night. The vision of Terezina was before my eyes. I was kissing her madly, then, she escaped from my arms, and I chased her madly through a pure-white meadow, white with snow. I twisted and turned in bed, haunted by the vision. At the break of day, I was at the bar. The very first customer.

The barman was amazed at seeing me there so early.

"I said in the morning, Greek, but I didn't mean at the crack of dawn! Where did you spend the night? On the sidewalk?"

"I slept on my bed," I replied, "but my sleep was restless and tormented."

He sat on the chair Terezina had been sitting on the night before, wheezing like an old engine and said, "Greek, I know what your trouble is. I was once in your shoes. When my hair was as black as yours and I was hale and hearty. But the little peach that has driven you crazy since yesterday is not for you. Pull yourself together, Greek, because between you and me, I would be very sorry to hear that your handsome young body had been found, riddled with gun-shot, on a New York sidewalk.

"What makes you say that?" I asked, really scared.

"Because a fellow made up to the girl once, and the next morning I saw his face on the paper..... Get me?"

"What I get is that I must keep off Terezina. Is that it?" I said.

"That's right. You're a smart one," said the barman.

"Do you mean that Terezina bumped off that poor chap?"

"I don't believe she did it with her own hands. But someone did it for her. Now mind you, that's only guessing. But what seems strange to me is that girl scatters money all over the place, heeds no one, drinks like a fish, goes with whoever she fancies, and there's no one to warn her off what she's doing. When that ritzy-rich woman comes to fetch her, the one I mentioned to you yesterday, Terezina goes for her like anything, she calls her such dirty names, that I wonder how she puts up with it."

"Getting to the bottom of all this and clearing up the mystery is going to give us something to do till my ship calls in again. Let's have a sandwich now; we don't want Terezina to come and find us famished."

"Greek, I've warned you. Take care."

"Okay," I said, "I can look after myself, don't worry..."

But the day wore on, and Terezina didn't appear.

"Do you think she will come?" I asked the barman for about the hundredth time. In the meantime, he and I had become friends, and I had eaten up nearly all his sandwiches.

"She'll come," he said, "she's bound to come.

She did come. She came about nightfall, when it was getting dark outside. She was even more beautiful, more desirable. But from what

I gathered, she was even thirstier than the night before. The barman rushed towards her, and started asking her questions:

"Terry, where have you been all day? What's happened to your friend, the posh lady? Merry Christmas, Terry, and a Happy New Year"…..

"I only feel at home here," she said.

Then, she sat at her usual table, and I heard her say, "First of all, bring me a bottle of champagne, the oldest and the best you've got. Then, follow it up with brandy and whisky. I'm treating everyone tonight……"

He looked at her sorrowfully.

"Are you going to drink again tonight, my little Terry?"

"Don't start your whining, Boy, you know I can't stop now. Nothing can make me stop….. Especially now….."

"And your friend, the fine lady, what does she say?"

"She used to say. Now she can't say anything, she's dead. They saw it that she died."

The barman laughed, thinking it a joke. "You do tell some morbid jokes!"

He wiped his hands on his apron and went to the counter to get her order ready.

"If you ever see her again," she called out, "you have the right to shit on me."

He came to her with champagne. He opened it laughingly. He filled two glasses and gave her the one.

"Merry Christmas, Terry!"

"Merry Christmas, sir." You could see they were both moved.

"Terry," he said, "I don't want to spoil your evening, but just listen to what I've got to say. Look at all these people here. They come every day, have a glass or two, and then they go back home at night."

"Whereas I forget to go back home," she interrupted.

"Yes, you forget to, Terry," he went on, "You shouldn't, you know, you're still a child. Tell me what's making you so miserable, maybe I can help you."

"Where do they go after their drink, sir?" she asked.

"Home, Terry, to their folks, to their families."

"Very good, sir, so much the better for them. But I have no family, I have no folks, I have no home. I have a house, but it doesn't belong to me only. It belongs to all who can pay well."

"Don't tell me you've got no family. How did you come into the world?"

"I came from Heaven, along with Christ, but something happened on the way and I was delayed, so I stayed behind....."

"Listen, Terry..."

"I'm not going to listen to anything. Tonight is the eve of one of the birthdays of my friend, Christ. I'm going to celebrate. Do you know why? Because we've both been crucified. Only he got on his own back and became famous; whereas, I'm still unknown."

She lifted her glass and swallowed its contents in one long gulp. Then, she re-filled it again. The barman was watching her in amazement.

"Why are you looking at me, sir? I'm Terry the drunkard, the little tart who has often kicked up a fuss in your bar. You used to send me packing, why don't you do so now? Oh, don't worry, my aristocratic friend won't bother you again. You can send me away if you like, sir, but I won't go. I'm used to insults, just as I'm used to boozing in your dive. Besides, I've got memories. I warn you, sir, if I can't leave your bar some night, let me sleep here in a corner. Throw me into a corner like an empty sack, but for God's sake, don't call the police. For your own good, sir, I'm telling you this because I love you. I swear to God I've never seen, that I love you."

"Terry, the only reason why I've ever sent you packing was because I love you, it was to stop you drinking too much. As your friend the grand lady, I don't know what has become of her, but whether she comes here again or not, you're to stay, no one will harm you, that I promise..."

"She was a real grand lady," she broke in, "I swear she was."

It seems a tear ran down her cheek unchecked, for I saw him wipe it away with the cloth he was holding.

"What are you wiping there, sir?"

"Your tears."

"Really, was I weeping? How funny. A whore's tears on a barman's cloth. It's a good thing, sir, they didn't drop it into my glass and water my drink. To your health, sir."

"Why are you always so hard on yourself, Terry? Listen to me..."

"Leave me alone, sir. That's my way of forgetting, in bars. Until someone remembers me and comes and picks me up; but now, there's no one to come and pick me up, Mammy who used to is..."

There was a lump in her throat. She lifted her glass. The barman dried another tear with his cloth.

"Let me drink, sir; let me drink. Because if I don't, I'll go crazy. Fill up all the glasses, sir, bring me all the bottles, let me drink. If I drink, I may stop thinking, I may lose myself. Our life is loathsome, sir, dirty, full of despair, full of disaster, disaster and despair, nothing else."

If you ask me what I felt, listening to that harrowing talk, I'd say that at that moment, I was more dead than alive. I felt my heart bleed. I was convinced that this ethereal creature was unbearably, unbelievably unhappy. Why should such a love be my lot? Why?

That's the common cry of all who are persecuted by ill-luck.

"Terry," said the barman in a sad voice, "do you see that young fellow over there?" She raised her eyes. She saw me.

"The Greek," she said. "A handsome chap. I remember him."

"He's a seaman, he's left his ship for a while. In ten days' time, he'll be sailing again. Meanwhile, he's all alone in New York. Do you want to keep him company? He speaks a little English, and you know a bit of Greek, so you'll get on fine. You'll keep each other company over Christmas, and you can talk about Greece."

He was keeping to our agreement. He was trying to ease her pain. He was offering her someone to help break the monotony of her life. She loved that barman she called 'Boy' when she was drunk. He was one of those kindly Americans, those rough diamonds that have not been spoilt by the cunning Europeans. Once he had said that his grandfather had been an Indian, and when she was joking with him she used to call him 'Indian', but that was not when she was tipsy. When she was drunk, she called him 'Boy', or 'Old bastard' or 'Old sod'. That evening, she was not tipsy, so she said laughingly: "Okay, Indian, call my fellow countryman."

He laughed, too. "I love you, Terry." he said with feeling.

"Stop being sloppy, Indian, and call the Greek before I get tight."

"John," "he called, "come over here."

"He's better looking tonight. All the Greeks are fine-looking fellows. That makes me feel so proud. Terry, don't let me be friendly with Greeks. He's afraid. I know what he's afraid of, and because I'm afraid of Terry,

I avoid them. But tonight? Tonight I'm not afraid of anyone. Tonight, Indian, you've given me the finest present of the year…

You've given me a handsome Greek for company. I love you, Indian," she said.

I went near her, a glass of beer in my hand. "Good evening," I said, my voice was deep and merry. A clear voice that came from a young and healthy chest.

"Good evening," she said, looking at me appraisingly. "Your eyes are blue, Sailor, the color of the sea that bathes our Greek coasts. Is it true that Greece is as blue as your eyes?"

"Still bluer," I answered, blushing.

"John, Terry is Greek too," said the Indian, for want of something better to say.

"I've known that since yesterday," I said. "Were both your parents Greek?" I asked with childlike directness.

"Yes," she answered.

"And your name is Terezina."

"Yes, and yours is John."

"So you remember me?" I asked joyfully. I felt as if I had just been given the prize.

"Yes, I remember you. Sit down."

I sat down opposite her. Only then did I realize that the barman had moved away. He knew that he was no longer needed. He just smiled at us from a distance.

"Do you know the Indian, John?"

"I've known him since yesterday, when I got to know you, too."

"I've known him for a year. I'm one of his most regular customers. I'm a pain in the neck for him sometimes, but somehow, he puts up with me."

"You speak Greek well," I said, ignoring the 'pain in the neck'.

We spoke to each other in an unrestrained way, without any affected politeness. We had met in a bar, so we carried on in the same casual way.

"No, I don't speak it very well, but it's the language I'm doing my utmost not to forget."

"Have you been in the States long?"

"About six years. I told you so yesterday."

"Yes, you're right, you did tell me. What brought you here?"

"I was washed ashore from a wreck. To your health, John. And listen, if you want to keep company with me, stop asking questions. I won't ask you any either. Questions kill our fleeting joy, and spoil the atmosphere. Put that glass of beer down, now we're drinking champagne."

"Just one more question, Terezina." I insisted.

"Well, if it's only one let's hear it."

"Why do you drink so much?"

"To grow tall and strong like you."

"When do you stop drinking?"

"When I'm asleep. But I sleep very little, so that means I drink a lot. What part of Greece do you come from, John?"

"From Rhodes."

"Is it beautiful?"

"Yes, very beautiful."

She read the homesickness in my eyes. "So you've been away six years?"

"I've been away for eleven years, but I went back on a visit six years ago. This year, I had planned to go back again, but things didn't turn out as I had expected. Six years ago, at Christmas, I was having a fine time at home, in Rhodes. We were having a real Greek party, and were enjoying ourselves as only Greeks know how to enjoy themselves..... As I was on shore, I thought of going to one of those Greek joints here in New York, but the good places are all so expensive....."

"I would like to enjoy myself as the Greek do, just for once," she said. "Two years ago, a friend of mine had taught me a Greek dance. It's called the Sirtaki. So as not to forget it, I bought a record of the music, and I dance it when I'm in the mood. I remember all the steps well."

"Do you really know how to dance the Sirtaki, Terezina?"

"Do I indeed.....just try me!"

"If only I had two hundred dollars, just for tonight." I said with a sigh.

"What would you do if you had that money?" she asked with a smile.

"Can't you guess? We'd go somewhere to dance the Sirtaki. I've got about that much money in my pocket, but that has to last me the rest of the month."

She read the regret on my face and in my eyes. The regret that shows on the faces of all young men who cannot fulfill their dreams and their wishes because of lack of money.....

"John," she said, "would you be my guest this evening? We'll go any place you like, we'll dance and have fun, even if its costs us a thousand dollars. I'm Greek, and the Greeks are hospitable, so you'll be my guest."

"It's true that the Greeks are hospitable, Terezina."

"Hospitable and ambitious, the bastards," she said.

She was my hand shake, and instead of taking my glass to my lips, it split all over the front of my jacket.

"Terezina!" I said reprovingly.

"Hush, not a word." she said. I know lots of dirty words, and you must know them, too. If you didn't, you wouldn't be much of a seaman, would you? So let's go and spend a thousand dollars."

"A thousand dollars. I travel the high seas for a year to save up a thousand dollars, my little Mermaid."

"Don't you worry, I'll do the paying. You're a guest. When I come to Greece, it will be your turn."

"I can't bear the thought of spending your money. We Greeks don't put up with such things. It's the men who pay, not the girls, the opposite is considered shameful."

"Shameful!" she said. "That's a word I hear for the first time in my life, and it makes my stomach heave."

"Impossible," I said, "I can't let you pay."

"Don't be so proud," she said, "come, let's go. Where's your coat?"

"I've no coat, only a duffle jacket, and that's in a mess."

"Haven't you got another suit of clothes?"

"I have, but it's in a bundle under my bed in my room at the hotel."

"Alright, then, your duffle will do, so long as you don't feel cold."

"Where would you like to go, to the dance the Sirtaki, to smash a few plates, to have some fun? To enjoy ourselves like Greeks, to hell with two hundred dollars."

"We'll go into the first place we come across on leaving here."

"Okay, the first place we come across."

As we passed the barman, he looked at us with joy in his eyes,

"Sir," she said, "I forgot to drink my whisky. Keep it for tomorrow. Thank you, sir."

"Okay, Terry. Merry Christmas."

"Merry Christmas, sir. Thank you very much."

A HAPPY EVENING

The evening I spent with Terezina will always remain like a dream in my life. One blissful evening. A night that was a whole life.

We went to a Greek nightclub and got a table right near the musicians. Terezina ordered the most expensive champagne and the most expensive food. The waiters fell over one another in their eagerness to serve us. They even brought flowers to our table.

"You're beautiful tonight, Terezina." I said, looking at her fondly. "I'm ashamed of the way I'm dressed. I'm in my sailor's trousers and striped shirt, and you in your golden dress. What must all these people thinking? With your blonde hair spilling down your back and your wonderful blue eyes, you're like a Greek goddess, or rather, one of those Greek heroines one reads about in books, in history books, I mean, and their exploits fill one with admiration."

"I'm always beautiful, John," she said. "That's why I'm rich. Whoever said that beauty and wealth walk hand-in-hand knew what he was talking about. But this evening, I remembered that I am a Greek. Don't worry about that way you're dressed. You're more attractive and more of a man than that dandy over there who is staring at us, instead of eating the food that's piled up on his plate. Just look at him: he can scarcely breath because his collar and bow-tie are strangling him. John, I bet he's wearing a corset....."

She burst out laughing. We both laughed and laughed happily, like two school children who have played hooky and are proud of it. That night, I was alive. I didn't care if I died the next day.

"You, Greece, and I have eyes of the same color. The colors of Greece are blue and white, the colors of our flag… Is Greece beautiful, John?"

"The most beautiful country in the world. A land wafted by the wind. Caressed by the waves. Birds sing her wonders, her purple sunsets, her silvery stars. Legendary castles made her inaccessible. A glorious, unvanquished land. A land that has born brave men and beautiful women, heroes, demigods, gods. A land that has born you and me."

"Avanti Maestro, let's have a song, and don't anyone dare say a bad word about a seaman, a Greek seaman."

Terezina and I turned round to see who was speaking.

"Milto, you good-for-nothing rascal!" I cried as I sprang to my feet.

"John, you bastard," cried Milto.

We fell into each other's arms. We carried on like mad, just like two ten-years-olds who have won a school prize.

"What brings you here, you old swine?" asked Milto. "Who is that smasher who has been asking if Greece is beautiful? Why don't you give her an answer?"

"I didn't have time to answer." I said. "You horned in and told her everything there is to tell. Terezina is Greek. We have come here to spend the evening. Where have you sprung from?

Milto drew up a chair and sat astride it with his arms resting on his back. He, too, was a good-looking guy. Tall and dark, with brown eyes that were sly, yet playful. Eyes that have made many girls' hearts beats faster, in his various ports of call. He looked very much like a gypsy.

"I left my ship," he whispered in my ear, as he looked round cautiously, "I can't stand the sea any longer. The sea is fickler and more deceptive than any woman that had ever crossed my path. Unbearable, I say. The one moment the sea lulls you to sleep like a baby, and the next, you get such blows that you wish you had never been born."

"How did you manage to leave the ship?" I asked.

"The same way as last time. Just as we used to do when we were kids playing at pirates. Get me?" He pointed to his head with his fingers and laughed. "Now I'm going to look for a curvaceous negress, marry her, and produce about a dozen little blackies and go on living in this New World. But I must be careful the American gestapo doesn't get hold of me."

"The Immigration Service, you mean?" asked Terezina.

"Oh, Miss," he said, "Don't use such dirty words,. They should not pass your pretty lips, lips like rose petals, and I feel like kissing them."

I laughed. Milto was such a lady-killer, and he expressed himself so funnily.

"Terezina," I broke in, "don't take Milto seriously.

We've been friends since we were kids. We grew up together. We used to daydream of traveling all over the world in search of hidden treasure. We wanted to become pirates. But our plans didn't materialize. Because when Milto was fifteen years old, he fell in love with the washerwoman, and she got hold of all our savings. Afterwards, he fell in love with the cook. She prepared all sorts of goodies for his sake, and our pocket money went on the goodies; then, it was the turn of the tobacconist, then, the money went to hiring bicycles, and so on. So, instead of becoming pirates, we became seamen. And instead of coming back with a treasure after each voyage, we came back with two hundred dollars. He's the fellow who had ruined my life, may he get the punishment he deserves."

I shook my head dramatically. Milto gave me a pat on the back.

"Forgive me, John. But I was born with a weakness for the fair sex. Now I'll try to make amends for the harm I've done you. When I've found my negress, I'll get on in the world. I'll do my best to find you, too."

"For goodness sake, Milto, don't get me mixed up with racial discrimination and such problems." Our laughter rang through the saloon.

"Maestro, a sirtaki," called out Milto.

The musicians switched to a Sirtaki in no time. All three of us jumped to our feet. Terezina threw off her shoes. Milto and I were other side of her. The music struck up. Greece and Sirtaki. We jumped about full of joy, drunk by the music and dance.

"I love you Greece."

"I love you, my country."

"Oh, oh, oh, ah, ah, ah," shouted Milto, "I'm not going home tonight!"

"You've got no home, you silly idiot."

"I'll make one, oh, oh, whoopee!"

"Okay then, don't go home, ever," I cried.

"Nor will I," cried Terezina in her broken Greek.

"Maestro, faster, faster," I called.

Now, our feet had wings. The tables near the dancefloor were pushed back. We danced and danced, and the floor trembled. The people clapped. The music went on playing. The players were getting flushed and hot.

"Sirtaki, Greece and Sirtaki. I love you Greece. I love you, my country. I love you America, for making me rich."

I don't know how many times Terezina repeated those words that evening. That wonderful evening, that wonderful night. She hardly trod on the floor, she almost flew about. She threw her hair forwards over her face, then tossed it back over her shoulders. Her eyes shone like stars. Her cheeks were two bright red poppies. She slipped from my arms into Milto's, and we, in turn, knelt before her and kept time with the music by clapping our hands.

"Long live Terezina," I shouted, half mad with joy.

"Long live Greece and all her beauty," cried Milto.

"Long live today, and to hell with tomorrow," cried Terezina.

Milto pulled the tablecloth off the table, and down went everything, shattered to pieces. That was another joyful outlet. We lifted Terezina on to the table. She went on dancing there. She was like a rose in full bloom as she twisted and twirled and her skirt spread open as she spun round. I don't know how long she went on dancing. Time had come to standstill for us... Time and place. Life and death...

Milto and I lifted her off the table. We were perspiring and bright red, all three of us. The music went on playing other Greek dances. My heart was beating, as if to burst.

"Champagne." cried Terezina.

"There's none left, we spilt it as we were dancing," I said.

"Call for some more," she said

We looked at one another. She understood, the bill…

"Listen kids," she said, "I'm paying tonight. I don't care how high the bill goes. Let it go up to two or even three thousand dollars. So much the better. There's plenty of money in that bag of mine tonight. We'll spend it to the last penny."

We looked at one another again.

"Not a word from either of you," she said, "call the waiter. And listen, you poufs, I'm footing the bill. So come on, let's drink, eat, and be merry. But before we begin dancing, I want to tell you something: 'You must love whores, and tell them wha you are dreaming of."

"A hotel with a restaurant and a garage," said Milto. Joh will run the hotel and the restaurant, and I, handsome guy as I am will escort the ladies to the garage…

He winked at me slyly. I patted him on the back.

"Why, old pal, am I so ugly-looking then?"

"You're not ugly, but you're too modest. You can't forget you family tradition. All the men in your family are decen fellows. I remember your mother telling you that, as she lulled you to sleep when you were a babe in arms. You, my dear John, haven't got it in you to lead a girl astray. I committed that sin years ago, may God forgive me…

He made the sign of the cross in such a way as only my friend Milto, the old bastard, could.

"You are both good-looking guys," interrupted Terezina, "how much would you need to open such a hotel in Greece? We'll drive Onassis out of business, and as I dispose o youth and charm, I'll do my best to lure his adorable Jackie away from him."

"Now joking apart, I'm seriously interested in business," said Terezina.

"If you've chosen me as a business partner, then you've had it in advance, I'll play you false, as I did poor John. He, at least, had the sea to fall back on, but it won't be the same for you, that profession hasn't yet opened up to women, curse them. At least as sailors, we can still hold our own with pride....."

She laughed, she laughed out loud. As if she had just heard the funniest joke in the world. We looked at her like goofs.

"What are you laughing at?" we both asked in chorus.

"My villa is worth twice or three times that much," she said amid her laughter, "And if you are thinking of doing me out of the money, Milto, you're welcome to it."

Now we looked at her in even greater amazement.

"Terezina, please stop drinking," I said.

"John, I swear I'm not drunk... I've hardly drunk at all this evening. Tomorrow, Christmas Day, I'll make you both my partners, in exchange for the wonderful evening we've spent together....."

"It's out of the question, We can't accept," we replied

"I said we're to be partners," she shouted.

"Impossible!" I cried, "I won't have your money; it's you I want. You and only you. I love you and want to marry you."

"Who spoke about marriage?" the question escaped her before she had time to think.

"I did, and I repeat what I said: Will you marry me?" I spoke breathlessly, hurriedly, my chest heaving like the waves of the sea. I spoke as if I were afraid someone else would say the words before me.

She did not move; she stood like a pillar of salt. The color left her cheeks, and her lips began to tremble. Milto seemed completely taken aback, I'd never seen him like that before.

"I love you, Terezina, I want to marry you," I repeated as I put her hand in mine.

I felt her hand tremble as I held it. It felt like a bird fluttering to get out of a trap, but while I was waiting for her answer, she suddenly sprang to her feet and then on to the dance floor.

"Sirtaki!" she cried, "Sirtaki!"..... Whoopee, Greece and Sirtaki."

Day began to dawn, but it was as dark as night in my heart as long as there was no answer to my proposal.

When we left the club, the day workers were already arriving.

"Terezina," I said, "Let's go somewhere where we can talk."

"You don't need me now, so I'll make myself scarce," said Milto." If you should need me, John, you know where to find me, I'll be waiting for you. Terezina, thanks for a wonderful evening, I'll remember it all my life, and mind, don't leave John by himself."

He stooped and kissed her on the forehead. Then, he walked away, head bent. He seemed troubled. I knew why, and now I needed my friend, I needed him so badly.

"Milto is a wonderful fellow, John," said Terezina.

"He's a fine person and a real friend. He has a heart of gold…"

"You don't know how glad I am, John, that you've got suc a kind and loyal friend."

"Terezina, I'm waiting for your answer….."

"Here in the street? Do you think it's the right place to tell the story of one's life?"

"Where shall we go then?" I asked.

"What about a walk through Central Park? It's marvelous there at this time of day, what with the song of the birds, and the children skating, and the music....."

"I've never been there before."

"We'll go now....."

When we got to the park, we held hands and began to run in the snow until we reached the first little hill. We sat on a large stone.

"Gee, it's wonderful here," I said, "Terezina this is a real paradise."

"Didn't I tell you so!"

"Well, Terezina, I don't blame Milto for wanting to stay in this country, I think I'll do the same."

She laughed.

"So, do you want to hear my answer, John?" she asked.

"Terezina," I said, "Look at those trees laden with snow, decorated for Christmas. Look at those children running about. Look at the sun, trying to shine through the branches of the snow-covered trees. Look at the clouds in the sky.

Look at the high buildings, the people coming and going. All that, Terezina, is life. Life that is very dear to me. Life that belongs to every human being, that belongs to you and me. Our meeting yesterday was indeed strange. I know nothing about you, about your life. But I don't want to know anything. You asked me not to ask any questions, I promised not to, and I'm going to keep my promise. I don't care what you did yesterday, or the day before, or all the years that have gone by... But there is pain and sadness in your eyes. "Tell me, please, tell me something..."

"What makes you say all that John? Why should you care about my life?"

"However ridiculous it may seem, I'll tell you Terezina. Since our meeting last night, I have had the feeling that I've known you for years. I love you, I love you as if I had loved you all my life. From the very day I was born. I am poor, but that is of no importance, poverty is not a disgrace. I'll go on working as a sailor for a few more years, and you will have everything you wish. And as you said, your family is not interested in you, that means we don't have to worry over getting their consent..."

All the time I was speaking, she was looking at me as if fascinated. She had fallen in love with me, too. She was in love for the first time. But how was that? During one evening in a lousy dive? How could such a tender feeling be born?

She had known so many men, but they were part of her job, she had not loved a single one of them. She was always in a hurry to sell them her love, collect her fee, and be off. Whereas now? Now, she had been caught. My blue eyes had got the better of her.

"John, when you hear about my life, you'll loathe me," she spoke softly and slowly. "You'll hate me. However much you love me, you must tear yourself away from me. For your own good. The feelings of my heart can't alter things. If by burying myself alive I could change things, I would gladly do so.

But I will not drag you into my sordid life. Now all is over.

Yesterday is finished. I'm not a woman to live with one man.

I go with lots of men. I'm a whore. A drunken harlot. A dope

peddler. I'm corrupt, I can't have children…"

I looked at her, I listened, and laughed.

"I told you I don't care a damn about your past. All that I care about is the present, this minute, and this minute you are Terezina, the girl I love. What if you can't have children, we'll adopt as many as we like. What is of importance is that we're in love with each other, nothing else matters. I'll take you with me on my ship, she sails in ten days' time, and we'll go to Greece. I love you, can't you understand that? Why do you want to send me away from you by using all those slanderous words against yourself? To force me to leave you? A whore wouldn't have such a heart of gold. You're an angel, Terezina."

"There are no angels on earth, John, I'm really and truly a whore."

"You're a little girl that has drunk more than is good for her."

"I'm beginning to worry about you."

"Don't worry about me. I love you. Don't think I want to marry you for your money. I'll put a match to all your money and burn it. I'm young and able to work. I'll earn money. I've been a seaman for eleven years. I've got a house in Greece, a real little palace, I'll take you there to live..."

"If you don't believe me," she said, "go to the bar where you met me yesterday, ask the barman, and he'll tell you what sort of woman I am."

"You're wrong again," I said, "I asked him yesterday, lon before we spoke to each other, when you were sitting alone at that little table. And he told me you're the kindest person that ever set foot in his bar."

"I'll push his bloody face in," she shouted angrily, "The dirty liar, the old bastard."

"So Terezina!"

"Now I feel that the ground is sliding away from under my feet. Central Park, that was so beautiful a short while ago, has now become a hell I cannot escape from. Listen, John. For the first time in my life, the birds are singing in my eighteen-year-old heart. For the first time, I've come to realize what I am... So I'll tell you what I am: I am a source of income in the hands of a notorious, unscrupulous pimp, who is the terror of the New York Underworld. And not only that, but he is feared by the police as well. I can't break away from his clutches, and I don't want him to cause you any harm. Because... (she stammered) because I love you, John. I haven't loved you since yesterday, but since I was a little girl of twelve and had every right to dream of the future. But now I no longer have that right, John..."

She burst into sobs and ran away from my side. I was disconcerted for a moment, but only for a moment. In my mind and in my heart I only retained the meaning of one thing she had said. She loved me. I was happy.

"Terezina," I shouted, running after her like one possessed. I caught up with her, took her in my arms, and holding her little face cupped in my hands, I smothered her with kisses.

"I adore you, my darling," I said.

"Yesterday is dead. A new day has dawned for us."

"Yesterday is still alive, John. It's not dead, and it will live as long as I do."

"I will not have you say such things, my love, Don't call down curses upon yourself. Now I love you ten times more. We'll get married, we'll go far away, and you'll forget the past. I swear I'll do everything in my power to make you forget, my sweet one."

A ray of sunshine played on her fair hair, and I think it reached her heart. Her smile will forever remain branded on my memory, like a scar on my flesh.

LOVE KNOWS NO BOUNDARIES

"Let's get married, John, I think I have the right to a few hours of happiness."

I was too happy at the moment to notice the bitterness in her voice. If I had noticed, if only I had noticed.....

But even if I had, how could I have stayed the course of destiny? The ill fate of my beloved?

Tell me, how can one avoid a disaster that approaches soundlessly and unexpectedly?

"Come on, let's" was all I said.

We went into the first jeweler's shop we came across.

"Two wedding rings," I said to the jeweler, with a victorious air.

When I placed the ring on her finger, she burst into tears again. Without saying a word, I stooped and kissed her. Those tears were tears of joy, and I was happy to see her shed them.

"You are mine now, my love. Mine and only mine."

"I'm yours forever," she said, and then she added, "I've got money to pay for the rings."

Without answering, I took her handbag. I furiously grabbed all the money there was in it, down to the last penny. Then I asked the jeweler for a sheet of paper and wrapped all the money in it.

"How much do the rings cost?" I asked, and paid for them with my own money. "In my country," I said, "the man pays for the wedding rings."

On leaving the shop, I took the money I had wrapped in the sheet of paper, and when we were in the street, I tossed it as far away as I possibly could. Terezina watched me.

"Why are you looking at me like a booby?" I asked. "Yesterday is dead. That money will remind you of the years I want you to forget. From this day you are mine, and I'll pay for anything you need."

For the first time, she put her arms around my neck. For the first time, her lips touched mine.

Dear God..... Dear God..... Where had you been hiding such happiness for me? In the middle of a busy street?

At the first public telephone, we stopped to ring up Milto.

"Come over here, I'm getting married. I want you to take us to that priest you know of."

He must have swallowed his tongue, for no sound came over the wire, so I had to shout into the phone,

"I'm getting married, idiot. I'm getting married, and I need that friend of yours, the priest. And make it snappy!"

I just heard him say, "I'm coming." Then, I rang off.

A STRANGE WEDDING

The priest was a pensioner. An old fellow who could hardly walk. When we got to his small apartment in a street of Astoria, and we told him what we had come for, he nearly had a stroke.

"But my children, weddings are held in the town hall or in a church."

"The words they use there can be used here by you," I said stubbornly.

"But…" he protested.

"There is no 'but' about it. You've got to marry us. Here is our best man; he is a friend of yours, Milto, who saved you from drowning when you fell into the sea at Piraeus, and didn't know how to swim. Now, the time has come to show your gratitude—he saved your life, don't forget!"

"We need the necessary papers." he protested.

"Fiddlesticks!" I said, "Here's a piece of paper, write on it saying that you've married us and sign it. When we get to Greece, we'll have a proper wedding."

"Okay, then," he consented.

"We'll pay you for your trouble."

"I don't want any money," he said.

"If you won't take any money, so much the better, it's your duty to marry us."

"John," I said. "John Moschakis."

"John Moschakis," he repeated, "will you have Terezina as your wedded wife?"

I said, "Terezina, the family name?"

"There is no family name," said Terezina.

"What!" cried the priest. "What do you mean there is no family name?"

"I mean there's none. There was one once, but I've forgotten it," replied Terezina.

"She's forgotten it," I told him. "She told you she's forgotten it. Just write Terezina, and when she remembers it, you can fill it in."

I felt sorry for the poor old fellow. He looked flabbergasted. Finally, he said, "Alright. Terezina. Will you have Terezina as your wife?"

"I will," I replied. "I will have her as my wife beyond life and death. I swear to protect her, to love her, and to worship her. My heart, my soul, my very life I place in her hands."

The priest was trembling. Milto had bent his head, not for me to see the tears in his eyes. Terezina was standing perfectly still, like a wax doll. She was listening and squeezing my arm to keep from falling.

"Terezina," said the priest, "will you have John Moschakis as your husband?"

She was thoughtful for a moment. Then she said,

"I want him as companion of my joyful hours. I want him to be gay and happy. I want his days to be as bright as the sun, and his nights as serene as the moon. I swear to give my life for him. I swear... (a lump in her throat seemed to choke her) I swear to...to...even to kill for his sake."

The priest made the sign of the cross, He joined our hands. He read the blessing. Then, he wrote out something on a sheet of paper and gave it to me. I took it and pushed it. into my pocket, without even reading it. I kissed my wife, and then, with my arm around her, we walked out of the apartment.

In the street, we heard a voice calling to us.

"You wanted my company as long as you needed me!"

"Well we don't need you now, do we?" I said.

"That's what I say, you don't want me any longer, I'm in the way. So, I'm off in search of the great love of my life."

"Good luck," I cried.

In my hotel, I looked at my watch angrily; how fast it ran! It was already getting dark. The happy hours we had spent in each other's arms, Terezina and I, had sped away so quickly. I turned and looked at her cuddled up in my arms, and I thanked God from the very depths of ay soul.

I fell asleep happily. But I must have slept heavily, because when I woke, Terezina was no longer by my side. I called her. No answer. Frantic with anxiety, I ran to the reception desk to make inquiries.

No one had seen Terezina, my wife. Panic-stricken, I ran towards the only place where I could get news of her. I ran to the bar. And at the bar, my dreams were turned to dust, when the barman gave me the newspaper. Now, I hate newspapers more than ever.

THERE IS NO HAPPINESS UNMINGLED WITH SORROW

I found her that same day, behind iron bars. And it was Christmas Day. The blackest Christmas of my life. But in her, I did not recognize my rebellious and noisy Terezina. This was but a sallow, untidy girl with dark circles under her once lustrous eyes. Her lips were colorless, and her general appearance was that of a poor little broken bird. You could only tell she was alive by the movement of her eyes.

"John," she cried, gripping the bars.

"Terezina," I said.

A policeman unlocked the door. I rushed in and clasped her to my heart, as if I had not seen her for years. I stroked her hair and kissed her.

"Why, Terezina? Why?"

"I had to John." She suddenly drew away from me. "Now, my love, everything has changed. You'll hear such things about me, that you will come to loathe me."

She repeated my name again and again, as if she found comfort doing so.

"Nothing has changed. Nothing will ever change. Our life began yesterday, it will carry on from yesterday. You're my wife. Have you forgotten the promise we gave to each other?

I'll be by your side, I'll protect you, even if it means giving my life for you. I'll wait for you to come out of prison. My love, I'll never desert you."

I made her sit down. I took her hands in mine and kissed them and held them to my heart.

"Terezina, mind you tell your lawyer the whole truth about that man,"

I said, "I'm going to find you a lawyer. I'll get two or three or even ten, if necessary. We must get you off, my love.

"Lawyers cost money, John, and you won't touch my money."

"I've got some money put by, and if need be, I'll sell my house in Greece."

"No," she cried out, "Never, I'm not worthy of so much love or of such a sacrifice. I'm not worthy, I tell you."

"Don't you love me, Terezina?"

"I adore you, John, and that's why I'm speaking to you like this. I'm quite unworthy of all you have given me and are still willing to give me."

"You are not unworthy, my darling, Because you are honest and good."

"I'm neither honest nor good. I'm vile and bad. If I were not, I wouldn't take people's lives by selling them dope or by shooting them."

"Don't you value my life? Without you, there is no life for me. Think that over."

"Your life is before you, John. Your life will continue, even when I am no longer near you. Even when I am no longer of this world. Life is yourself, John. My dearest, my beloved John…..But I've got money, John, And I must pay to get myself out of the shameful mess I am in."

"You've got no money," I shouted, beside myself with rage.

"You've got nothing and nobody but me. I will pay for everything, I and only I."

"Yes, John, you are right, you are all I have."

"Will you help the lawyer, Terezina?"

"I will," she agreed.

"Tell me, what you would like me to bring you?"

"Nothing," she said, "I only need you, but you'll be taken away from me in a few days' time. Your ship will be sailing soon."

"To hell with my ship. To hell with all the ships in the world. I will be here with you day and night. Here by your side. Don't let that out of your mind for one moment."

"That thought will keep me alive, John."

AN UNEVEN STRUGGLE

She had promised to live with the thought that I would always be by her side. It seems she had not the strength to do so. She hadn't he strength to keep her word or the promise she had given me to help her lawyer and herself...

Peter, the policeman, and I had come to an agreement. And when the visiting hours were over and it was time for me to leave, Peter would stay with her.

We tried to convince her, day by day, that she would be acquitted. That a new life would dawn for her.

She would give us no answer. She would look at us like a stray dog looks at the person who has brought it in from the street. Neither she nor I ever spoke about her past again. We left that to the lawyer. She agreed to have a lawyer just to please me. She answered his questions without making any special effort to justify herself. On the contrary, the way she put things, she seemed to be entirely to blame.

The lawyer was at a loss how to make her realize that she had to give him some clue that he could use in her favor. When he persisted too long, she would get furious and show the worst side of her character.

"Shall I tell you something, lawyer? You are getting to be a pain in the neck. You keep on asking me the same old questions again and again. What the hell! Are you such a bloody idiot? How many times must I tell you the same things? Must you keep on at it? You're trying to get me off scot-free, but I am telling you once and for all: I killed him, I killed him, I killed him. It's beyond me how you ever managed to get that degree of yours; you're such a perfect moron."

The lawyer didn't seem to take offense. He would look at her and laugh heartily, as if she were handing out the highest of praises...

"Terezina, I'm asking you the same questions over and over again, because I want to help you," he would say. "I want to find some extenuating circumstances to strengthen your defense. Try and understand that, please, Terezina."

"I understand," she threw at him, "you bribed your professors to get your degree. You paid to get it."

The lawyer sighed in despair.

"You are right, Terezina, I paid to get my degree. I paid a high price to get it. I worked my way through college. I worked to pay for my food, my clothes, my rent, my books, my college fees."

"Bullshit!" she broke in, "Go get drowned, you and your rent and your clothes and your college fees. Leave me in peace, and never set foot in here again. Whenever you come here, I get a headache, so you'd better have a few aspirins in that briefcase of yours, besides those lousy books and all those bloody papers. So, now, get lost. I can't find peace, even in jail." She sighed.

"Okay," agreed the lawyer, "I admit I tire you, but you mus know it's all for your own good."

"Ha, ha, ha," she laughed rudely, "next you'll be saying that you are making a great sacrifice for my sake. Well, that's a bit too much, blast you," she said as she threw the comb she had in her hand, to the other end of her cell. Then, she got to her feet and began pacing up and down in front of the lawyer, whose patience was endless.

"For my own good, did you hear that?" she shouted. "For my own good, what good, you sissy? You mean for the good of your own pocket, that's where John's money is going, isn't it? Into your pocket…"

Her eyes seemed to be giving out sparks, her hands were Trembling, and her lips were twisted into a crooked grin.

"Damn you and all your kind who are supposed to be working for my good. Poppycock and fiddlesticks! You're telling me! I don't swallow that stuff. I've heard that sort of yarn too often. And listen, you bastard, I wasn't brought up in a convent, put that in your pipe and smoke it, I know what goes on around me, I've seen more than you have, I bet."

"I daresay you have," said the lawyer with a sad smile.

"Now get out of here, you son of a bitch," she cried.

"How do you know my mother was a bitch?" he asked.

"You don't have to be very smart to guess that. A queer like you couldn't have but a whore as a mother."

"Well, let's say that my mother was a whore. Haven't you, yourself, said that whores are as sharp as needles? So you are as sharp as a needle, and so am I. Only you don't know how to act smart. Instead of defending yourself and standing up for your case, you are doing your best to ruin everything. That's no being smart, that's being downright stupid."

He was doing his utmost to force her into telling him something that he could use at her trial to prove her innocence. But that only made her madder than ever.

"Bugger you and your arguments. Get out of my sight. If you had my good at heart, next time you come here, smuggle a bottle of booze in that briefcase of yours, or else don't dare show your lousy face in here again, or I'll tear you to pieces."

"If I bring you drink, you'll let on."

"I promise I won't say a word."

"Think of poor John. He's half out of his mind with worry, he'll soon be a human wreck."

"Can you bring me some booze?" she insisted, as if she hadn't heard what he had said.

The lawyer realized that she was beyond reasoning with. She wasn't speaking now, but her bad, poisoned blood. She was a victim of the bottle. But he made a last effort: "Terezina, I'll try and get you into a nursing home, where you'll have special treatment to cure you of this thirst for drink."

What on earth made him mention the word nursing home! Her beautiful face became distorted. Her features were altered. She went a peculiar bluish color. She was like a wild animal, ready to attack him and claw him to pieces.

"Out of here you flab, you sod, you son of a bitch. Get lost. Out, out, out."

What could he do? He hurriedly gathered up his papers and left the room, shutting the door behind him. And he was just in time to escape Terezina's shoe, which she sent flying after him. He stood outside the door, dumbfounded. His thoughts in disorder. He took out his handkerchief and wiped the sweat from his brow. He felt tired, beaten. He had failed once again.

"She's sick," he muttered, "very sick, very wretched. Maybe if a priest had a word with her..... he might make her see reason. But she needs treatment, a nursing-home, medical care."

"What she needs is a good hiding."

He looked up. A wardress had spoken. The blood rushed to his head.

"She's foolish," he said angrily, "foolish and puzzling. Don't any of you dare to touch her, don't you dare…"

He walked away with slow heavy steps, He sank into the seat of his car.

"My God, my God!" he whispered.. He gripped the steering wheel hard.

"I must speak to the District Attorney," he muttered, "I must explain to him…"

"What are you going to explain to him?" I asked as I sat up from the back seat, where I had lain waiting for him.

He showed no surprise at finding me there. He was so used to my presence, but luckily, he did not mind my following him around.

"She's guilty, John."

"That's impossible," I said. I had been expecting the lawyer to tell me that the case was black against the dead man.

"SHE IS GUILTY, John," he repeated. "I'm sorry to have to tell You, but she is. Her remorse forces her to punish herself."

I interrupted with a movement of my hand, an American mannerism I had picked up in ports. I remained silent for a moment to ponder the matter.

"Lawyer, what is your opinion?"

"She is sure to get a few years in jail."

"Do you really believe it?"

"I'm sure of it, But it's not only that."

"What else then?"

"She is sick."

"Sick? What of?"

"Haven't you guessed? She's an alcoholic."

"Oh, my Goodness!"

"Now, it's up to you. Only you can persuade her to go into the hospital to have a treatment, if, of course, it's not too late. I'm a lawyer, not a doctor, so I can't say how much harm has been done already."

"You say it's up to me. But I am so taken aback that I can hardly think..."

My brain seemed to have stopped working and thinking clearly, and all I felt at that moment was a terrible numbness, mixed with disgust and despair. What a cruel story this girl's life was!

"But she's only eighteen," I at last managed to utter.

He nodded. He showed understanding and patience.

"You've got to be kind to her, and give her all the courage you can."

COURAGE, I thought. But who will give me courage?

"Do you think we should send priest to speak to her? He might do something."

"I can't say," I answered. "I don't know what is best. You do what you think right."

I AM AN ATHEIST

Terezina greeted the priest with a curt, "And what have you come here for?"

The priest was rather elderly, his face was kind, but his whole attitude imposed respect. He'd been told by the lawyer what to expect, so he did not show any surprise at the reception he got from Terezina. He thought it best to humor her.

He cleared his throat. "Humph. What do you think I've come for? I often come round to visit the prisoners. These women like to speak to me about their troubles and to ask for my advice. I just dropped in uninvited, to see if you would like to have a chat with me."

"These women are idiots," she answered, "idiots and fools."

"Bravo, Terezina," he replied with admiration in his voice, "I agree with you there, they are really rather foolish. They consciously make mistakes and then ask for advice... But apart from prisons, priests go everywhere."

"Yes, yes, I know," she interrupted, "they often turn up where they are least expected or wanted.

"It's simple, my dear, we just do our duty...

It seems the word "duty" struck badly on her ears, because she turned her angry gaze on him and let loose a flow of indecent language. "Listen, Preacher. You took the trouble of coming here to bother me. Well, I don't want you, so go away. And come back only for my funeral. Although I hate funerals, I'm afraid I'll have to be at my own. 'Unavoidable', as my idiot of a lawyer says."

"Why do you hate funerals? Terezina?"

"I think funerals should be avoided at all costs. Death is something natural. I don't say death can be avoided. Death may be horrible, but it's natural. Even if it scares us. But funerals? There is no sense in decorating the dead with flowers, and only speaking good of them. What drives me mad at funerals is the sad air everyone assumes in duty bound. That's pure hypocrisy, damned humbug, and I'm sure even you don't approve of it, nor your God either."

The priest didn't speak for a while. He stood thinking. He never expected such a reasonable argument from a person like Terezina.

"So now you can make yourself scarce, be off quietly an decently, just as you came," she said.

She was making an effort to be polite…

"I am tired, my dear," he said ignoring her last words. "Won't you let a tired old man rest for a while on this one and only chair?"

She reflected before answering, watching him cautiously all the time.

"Two minutes," she consented. "You can rest for two minutes, but mind you keep your mouth shut all the time."

He stretched out his legs, crossed his arms on his chest, and bent his head forward. His attitude was that of a really tired person. He shut his eyes and took on an air of complete indifference. Then she asked him, "Who sent you here?"

"God, my child."

"Now don't you start preaching to me." she said, "no preaching in here. Just tell me who sent you."

"I told you, my child, no one sent me. I came of my own accord."

"I'm not your child," she snapped.

"We are all God's children."

"Will you stop harping on all this stuff about God? What God and poppycock are you gassing about all the time," she burst out, "I don't believe in any God, in any religion. I'm an ATHEIST, an unbeliever, that's what I am," she sneered.

He smiled and said, "I don't care whether you are an atheist or not. What I care about at this moment is resting my weary legs. When I've rested them, I'll leave you."

He was trying to gain her confidence, feigning indifference at her anger. He felt overwhelmingly sorry for this girl, who, although only eighteen, was already old and broken.

"And what have we two got to speak about, Preacher?"

"We haven't got much to speak about, nothing of importance, only chit-chat, like for instance, did you ever go to school?"

"I often passed by the school building," she answered as she half lay on her narrow bed.

"How did you learn to read and write then?" he asked, feigning Admiration, in order to flatter her.

"My Derry saw to that. You see, I had to know how to read the names on the doors."

The priest avoided asking the question: Which doors?

"So, you've got a father!" he asked, as if in surprise.

"I had two," she said, holding up two fingers of her right hand.

One was my real father and the other one wasn't. My real father did me one good turn, and only one: he kicked the bucket, he went to Hell."

"Is a father's death a good thing?"

"It depends on what kind of father he is. Some fathers do good to their children only by dying."

"Do you mean that he left you a fortune?"

She laughed derisively. "Yes, he left me a fortune, or, rather, a legacy: his second wife, a whore! She sold me to my other father, and he made my life a hell on earth. And I put six bullets in his body and sent him as a present to the Devil, Are you satisfied now?"

He shook his head sorrowfully. "All this is very sad, my child, very sad indeed."

"Thanks for telling me," she said.

"Will you let me speak to you for a while, Terezina?" he asked her, imploringly.

"Will it be about God and his blessing?"

"Exactly."

"I told you: no God, no religion... I don't believe in the existence of any God, and I don't like shamming."

The priest's expression was one that only a priest can assume…

"Why are you looking at me like that? What have I done to you?" she asked. "My joys and my sorrows are my affairs, and

I'll keep them to myself. Nobody is going to know of them, and last of all you."

"Why should I not know of them?"

"Because you are human, so naturally you are a bit daft, and you priests like to pretend that you never make mistakes. As if priests aren't men! Men, those monsters your God created. He gave them the power to destroy, by endowin them with reason. Men, those insatiable creatures, always unsatisfied, always wanting more. Your God cursed them, and then like a fool, He sacrificed himself for them. Men who revel in horror, and then stretch out their hands in charity."

There was a strange look in her eyes, the look of one who has been humbled. While talking, she had been walking to and fro in her cell.....

He listened without interrupting her.

He is stronger than I, she thought, *stronger and more obstinate.*

Suddenly, she felt the desire to shatter his calm, unperturbed attitude.

Her bad intentions were cut short by his quiet voice, "What is your family name, Terezina?"

"I've got no family name, just Terezina."

"I didn't know that you belonged to the nobility," he said.

"Yes," she said, "I come from a long line of aristocrats. All were eithers whores, queers, drunkards, or pimps, and all sorts of underworld personalities."

"I can hardly believe you," he said.

"Well you'd better, I'm not joking. I'm talking seriously," she answered.

"It's a sin to speak of your ancestors in that way; you must not speak ill of the dead," he said.

"That was well spoken, it's a sin, it's as plain as the nose on your face that you are a sinner; so go and ask your God to forgive you and leave me alone, to Hell with…"

"And what about truth?"

"There is no truth."

"You are wrong there, Terezina."

"That's my business. My life is my own, and I can do what I like with it. Now I want you to get out, I'm fed up. Haven't you rested your old legs long enough? Get going."

"Shall I leave one of my books here with you?"

"Go drown yourself, you and your bloody books. You've taken advantage of my kindness, You asked for two minutes, and you've been here an hour."

"What will the people here think about you speaking to me like that, shouting and sending me away?"

"I don't care a damn what people think. So clear out and let's not have another word from you."

She turned her back on him, her golden hair covering her shoulders. He walked away, tears welling in his eyes. He, too, had been beaten...

A SMALL FAVOR

The day after the priest's visit, Terezina said to Peter, the policeman who came to see her every day, "Peter, I want to ask you to do me a small favor, and I hope it will be the last I shall ask of you."

"I'll do whatever you want, Terezina."

"You can't do whatever I want, but at least you can bring me a few sheets of writing paper and a pen."

He took them to her. Four days later, Terezina gave Peter some badly written sheets of paper saying, "Peter, will you please give these to the District Attorney?. Give them to him yourself, see that no one else gets hold of them."

Peter was surprised. "But why to the District Attorney, Terezina? You've got a lawyer. Why don't you give these papers to him? He will make use of what you've written down here, and maybe he will get you off with a lighter sentence."

"No, Peter, what I've written there isn't for my lawyer. It's for the District Attorney. He must read it, He must judge me without any witnesses influencing him in my favor, or by lawyers pleading my defense with moving speeches.

Peter could not refuse her this small favor. He realized it would be useless to plead with her. So, he took the papers and gave them to the District Attorney.

The District Attorney had been reading the story of Terezina's life for several days. Meanwhile, she was dying slow death in her dimly lit prison cell. She passed her time playing with a toy rabbit someone had given her for luck.

She did her best to forget the thirst that was parching her throat and making it hurt more and more every day...

"John... Peter... some drink, please, give me something to drink..." Those were the same words we heard as soon as we got to the prison to visit her every day. They broke my heart. But the prison regulations made it impossible for us to do what she asked. "Peter, John, something to drink," her voice was a sob, a prayer, a supplication, but we could do nothing. I would bow my head and walk away, down the long corridors and into the street while her weak voice echoed in my ears and drove me crazy. "John, just a little, a very little, why won't you give me a little? Don't you love me?"

She asked if I loved her! I not only loved her, but now I was seized by panic at the thought that I might lose her forever. I clenched my fists so tight that my finger nails cut into the palms of my hands.

"Why won't you give me a little?

How could I make her understand that by refusing to give her some drink I was going against my will. That visitors were searched very thoroughly before entering the prison. That it was against the law to give her drink…

I had one last hope, only one. What had she written to the District Attorney? When would he finish reading her badly written story? Because, as I had been told, Terezina had written all the secrets of her short life to the District Attorney. How could one go and say to a District Attorney:

"Hurry up, finish reading Terezina's life story." One couldn't. So, as I couldn't tell him to get on quickly, I cursed him, him and all the District Attorneys of this world, fellows who had never done me any harm. But when bad luck is at your heels, you feel that you have to blame somebody.

MR. DISTRICT ATTORNEY
THIS IS MY LIFE

Mr. District Attorney,

I killed him, Yes, I killed that man, on that cold snowy Christmas night. On the night that Christ was reborn, I took a life. I killed him by sending six bullets into his body. I blew him to pieces.

I saw his wide-open eyes filled with fear. I saw him stagger and fall dead.. I saw him spread out his arms, like the wings of a wounded bird, trying to find some support. I saw him crumble to the ground before me and wriggle like a landed fish. I saw him creep like a worm, reach my bare feet and kiss my toes, as if begging for mercy. I saw a red stream of blood trickle from the corner of his mouth, then a last convulsion, and he was still. Dead...

Then, I felt peace in my heart, for the first time in my life. How terrible that one should feel peace after killing. Mr. District Attorney, don't think I killed out of sadism, I'm not a sadist, I'm a professional... I did good by killing that man. And that was, and is, and always will be the only good thing I have ever done...

I know what you will say. It's bad to kill. Then there should be no wars and no quarrels. I had a quarrel with that man. So I was at war, and in a war, only the one side wins.

I know it is bad to kill. That's the way you want it, that's what's in the law books, But you must know that sometimes, a death is an act of charity.

I killed him, Mr. District Attorney, because he, too, had killed me in his way. He not only killed me, but turned me into a ghost. My death was worse than his. He died but once. I have been dying at his hands every day since he first killed me. He is dead now, and you can't judge him for his crime. But I, who knew of his crime, have passed sentence on him. I, one of his many victims, had my cruel revenge…

You have to judge me, however. I know the judgment will be difficult, with the accused alive end the accuser dead. Especially as the witnesses will be on the side of the dead man.

A dead man like Derry, who knew a lot of well-connected people, high society, as they say, usually has the witnesses for the defense on his side. Why? You will find the answer to that question, Mr. District Attorney, because the law is in your hands. In any case, I don't care about my sentence. I don't care about my life… All I care about is that you free men of the world should get to know a little of what takes place around you. Why I killed… How I became a prostitute and then a murderess...

Mr. District Attorney.

A flower doesn't open unless the sun shines upon it and warms it. A river doesn't flow, unless there is a slope in the ground, or unless it overflows...

If there was no wickedness, we would not speak of goodness. If there was no war, we would not speak of peace, If there was no Satan, Christ would not have come. If there was trust, there would have been no Crucifixion. If there was no wealth, poverty would vanish. If there was no hatred, crime would be wiped out....

There is a reason for everything. And I had a reason for killing that man.

You free men, you idealists, who believe in God when and as you like. You who blame the Jews and Judas, who speak of war and peace, of love and hatred. I want you to know why I killed. Don't think I'm after a lighter sentence. What I want is to convince you, as I am convinced, that a flower does not fade before its time, unless it is blown off its stem by an ill wind. A wind that blows it into a gutter to rot, where nothing can save it. Who is to blame? The flower that could not withstand the force of the wind, or the wind that blew up unawares?

It's very difficult to say, isn't it, Mr. District Attorney? I'll make no effort to hide my shame and disgrace. I will tell you everything… down to the most sordid details. I repeat: I don't care about my sentence. I don't care what opinion you will have of me. I don't care if you feel loathing or if you smile ironically. I don't even care if you are touched by this story. I don't care about anything. Because according to you and to your laws, I am a prostitute. A murderess. Even if I saved your child…

I mentioned the word 'laws', Mr. District Attorney. Really, are the laws always fair? But why should they be fair? Weren't they made by men? Are all men fair?

I believe that courts of justice are nothing but a game… a treacherous game devised by the great… A game always won by the players with the fattest bank accounts and the highest social positions.

You, who sit on the bench every day, have surely learnt to distinguish justice from injustice. Let me tell you, however, that I, too, have learnt to distinguish injustice from justice. There is such a difference between the two that I often wonder, here, in my dark cell, if justice does really exist or if it is just a bad edition of injustice.

I am eighteen years old. If I am not mistaken, after my trial, I may be sent to the electric chair, but if not, then I will be shut up in a reformatory, where the rats and the cockroaches have kinder feelings than the wardens and the reformers...

Memories are like distant friends. We are sad because they are far away. But I have to bring back my memories; you have to know the truth. Besides, from now on, memories will be my constant companions, not the wardresses who peep at me suspiciously through the little window.

As I have already told you, I am eighteen years old. I was born in a refugee hut where my parents lived after they had fled to Greece from Asia Minor. They were unbelievably poor and wretched. My mother never even set eyes on me. She died giving birth to me. So, you see, I was a lucky child from the very beginning of my life. I soon learnt that everything has its price in this world. My mother died of puerperal fever, and my father, poor lad, couldn't bear life without a woman at his side side, soon got himself a second wife. This time, he was rather unlucky in his choice.

To be rid of me, my stepmother had me put in an institution. There I became a number: I was known as number fifteen. I was never called by my name. I was simply number fifteen, and naturally, I soon got used to being called that. The wards we slept in were large, with white-washed walls, and our little cots were squeezed close to one another.

Our play-ground was covered with dark-colored cement. We little kiddies, pale-faced and sad, used to toddle about on unsteady legs. I tried to laugh and talk, but there was no incitement for laughter, and no one seemed to want to talk. All the little inmates appeared to be dumb and uncertain of their steps... They were like flowers cut off their stems. Buds that sprouted gaily in the Spring, only to die an untimely death by the cruelty of life...

The poor little children wasted away, unable to demand their rights and the punishment of those who had imposed such a cruel captivity upon them, depriving them of the freedom to enjoy life.

How many such criminals are free among us, Mr. District Attorney? But they are protected by law, especially when they make the necessary financial contributions to the right places. Most of them are unknown, so it's natural that you should take your hat off to them. They could be your colleagues or your friends. Why not? The law does not apply here. The only law that applies in such cases is the voice of one's conscience, if one has such a thing...

One dark and dreary morning, my step-mother came to fetch me away from the institution. In her opinion, I was old enough to fend for myself; I was already five years old. In those five years, I had never seen my father or my stepmother.

When I reached home, I was dumbfounded. Things were much worse than at the institution. There, we neither spoke nor laughed, but at least there was someone to smile at us occasionally. Besides, we each had a cot to sleep in. At home, no one spoke to me, no one smiled at me. A neighbor came round to have a look at me, she stroked my hair and said, "Poor little thing."

My stepmother had pointed to a corner in the room saying, "You are to sleep there. Take this blanket to keep yourself warm." The blanket was nothing but a tattered old rag. "You see we all live in this hut," she added,

"You, me, and your good-for-nothing father, who has been the ruin of me, blast him."

Then, she showed me a basin full of dirty clothes.

"Wash those clothes," she said, "and when you've finished, I'll show you where to hang them up to dry."

Naturally, I did not understand what she was talking about. At the institution, we never had to wash clothes.

"I don't know how to wash them," I said.

She looked at me angrily. "You'll soon learn," she said, "do you think this is the institution, where all the little bastards were treated like lords and ladies? Here, there is no one to wait on you. You'll have to do everything yourself. Tomorrow, you are going to start work."

"What's a bastard and what's work?" I asked.

"Ha, ha, ha," she laughed as she dropped on to the dirty, unmade bed. "A bastard is the child of a whore. As for work, you are to run errands for the neighbors, and you are to go to the greengrocer's round the corner and clean the vegetables. I've arranged everything with the greengrocer and his wife. I've already bought some things from them which I haven't paid for....."

"What's a greengrocer?" I asked.

"Don't you even know that? I see you hardly know anything, but never mind, you'll live and learn."

I went to the basin and began to dabble about in the dirty water. I don't remember if I washed those clothes.

I only remember that I spilled a lot of water all over the floor and my stepmother beat me with one of her thick shoes. I began to cry.

"Shut up, you little bastard," she said, "I didn't bring you here to have to listen to your wailing. Shut up, or else I'll put you outside," she added as she gave me another clout.

It was cold and raining outside. I felt scared, so I stopped crying.

My father saw me in the evening. My eyes were red from crying, and I was trembling from fright, hunger, and cold.

He didn't come near me. He just glanced at me indifferently, Saying, "You'll grow up to be pretty like your mother, whom you killed. You're an ill-fated child, a cursed child, a damned viper, and I loathe you. To Hell with you. See that you earn your own living, because I'm broke."

"I'm hungry," I wailed.

He turned to my stepmother.

"Now that you've brought this brat here, let's see how you are going to feed her." I didn't understand the meaning of his words.. "Hurry up and pull off my boots," he said.

"I'm hungry," I repeated.

"Pull off my boots," he yelled.

I tried to pull off his boots, but I couldn't. I hadn't the strength. He called me a useless bit of baggage, and he gave me a kick that sent me reeling into my corner.

I began to cry and to ask to be taken back to the institution, but they jeered at me.

"Go back," said my stepmother, "Go, and if they'll have you, you stay there for ever. But they won't take you back. I don't remember how many bloody papers we had to sign before they would let us take you away."

"I'm hungry," I said, once again.

"Shut up," cried my father. "We are going to teach you manners here, spoilt brat, don't you know it's rude to cheek your elders? And wanting to leave home! Whoever heard of such a thing! What do you say, my dear?" he asked my stepmother.

"You are right," she answered.

Then, they opened a bottle and began guzzling in turn, straight from the bottle. They went on drinking until the bottle was nearly empty, then they had a fight as to who would have the last swig.. My father swore at my stepmother, calling her a harlot and a lot of other names I can't remember.

That was my first day at home... A very happy day...

Unforgettable... As you can see, Mr. District Attorney...

As I learnt later, my stepmother's money had gone on drink and on horses. Both my father and she were great gamblers and drunkards.

As I grew older, my life became even harder. Although I did work.

In the winter, it was awful. There were holes in the floor, and mice used to come out at night. At first, I was afraid of them, but later, we got friendly, the mice and I. I would hold a crust of bread between my fingers and feed them in the dark, without my stepmother knowing. But first, I would eat my own share, what my step-mother used to throw to me. Very often, the mice would get into my hair. I liked that because it sort of warmed me. I liked it when they tickled me, too. I used to make believe it was a tender hand caressing me.

Until I was eight years old, my only friends were the mice. I can hardly remember one peaceful evening. Either my father or my stepmother would come home drunk. Then, they would start to bicker, and that would lead to a stand-up fight. I often got my share of the flying plates, because drunk as they were, their mark was not very sure. To get out of the way, I would hide under the big bed, and watch the fight from there, wondering which of the two would come out on top. My stepmother won most times. Then, she would open a bottle and treat herself to a drink. Sometimes, she would remember me and say, "Come on kid, have a guzzle to get over the scare you've had."

I didn't dare say no. Because I knew I would get a kick or a blow with the bottle. That's how I gradually learnt to drink.

All those years, I used to work at the nearby greengrocer's shop, and in the evenings, I used to wash my father's and my stepmother 's dirty clothes. Either of them used to pocket my earnings.

One morning, my father didn't get out of bed. I noticed that the wall next to his bed was spattered with blood. The doctor came and said that my father's stomach had burst from too much drink. That's how my father died...

For a few days, my stepmother kept to the hut. I thought that things would be quiet, now that one of them was gone...

I was mistaken. I little knew that now was the beginning of the real tragedy of my life. That I would first be dragged through the mire, to end up a murderess.

THE BEGINNING OF
CORRUPTION

I was eleven, going on twelve. One night, one cursed night, my stepmother came home from the booze shop, drunk. She had started going out to drink more often now. That night, she brought a drunken American with her.

It was past midnight, and I was asleep. As I never had a nightgown, I used to sleep in my ragged old slip. I put on my dress and sat in a corner, feeling the eye of the American fixed upon me. My stepmother picked up a bottle, lay on the bed, and began to drink. Once or twice, she got up and came near me.

"Here, little bastard, have a drink, or else I'll pull your hair out from the roots. Drink, I want you to get like me…"

I was scared, so I opened my mouth. She pushed the bottle in and forced me to drink. I drank a lot of that strong liquor, my throat burnt, it felt as if I had swallowed fire. I began to cry. The American laughed, so did my stepmother.

"Have a look at that girl," she said. "I'll make a great whore of her, and then she'll provide me with as many bottles of booze as I need."

The American got up, seized her by the arm, and threw her on to the beds. "Leave her alone," he said, "she'll learn in time."

She left me and began drinking again, until the big bottle was empty. He watched her drink, a cruel smile on his thick lips, and he watched me, too...

She turned to the American after she had drained the bottle dry. She smashed it on the dirty wooden wall of the hut.

"Give me yours, give me your bottle," she cried.

"No, I won't." he replied.

He spoke broken Greek, but he managed to make himself understood quite well. I thought that very strange, because I had never before heard that people could speak more than one language.

"No, I won't give it to you," repeated the American, as he pointed to the big, flat bottle with the colored label...

She staggered to her feet, her eyes bloodshot and her lips distorted by rage. She picked up the big water jug from the table, and sent it crashing to the floor. The water made little puddles on the earthen floor, and some trickled towards me. I didn't stir; I was too scared.

"Give it to me," she cried again, "give me that bottle."

He laughed out loud, showing his pure white teeth.

"What will you give me for this bottle?" he asked.

Without answering, she quickly began to undress, tearing off her clothes in desperate jerks...

"Give me the bottle and let me drink. Then, you can have me."

She stood before him, stark naked. My heart was thumping wildly. I was trembling as I saw her standing there in front of me and the American, with no feeling of shame. I don't know why I was trembling—was it because she was naked, or because I was scared? I tried to keep my teeth from chattering.

I wanted to get out of the muddy hut as soon as possible. I turned towards the door; the American was blocking my way. I heard him laugh again. A harsh, cruel laugh. He did not take his eyes off me...

"What am I to do with you?" he sneered at my step-mother. "You stink of the grave, you old hag! Look at your sagging bosom, your bulging tummy, your flabby behind!"

Her glance was venomous. "That's all I have to give you...."

The American picked up the bottle and brought it to her lips. The smell of the liquor drove her mad. She tried to snatch the bottle from him, but he pulled it away in time.

Then, she slipped and fell on the wet floor, and her body was covered in mud. She moaned and writhed like a wounded animal, then she crept under the table and began to sob. "If I give you ten bottles, what will you give me?" asked the American.

"I've told you I've got nothing else," she wailed as she pointed to her mud-spattered body.

"You have got something else," he said, "but I don't know if you will give it to me."

"I'll give you anything you want, only let me have a drink..."

"Are you sure you'll give me anything I ask for?" insisted the American.

"Anything, anything..." she answered.

Her need for a drink was making her quake all over. "I want your daughter," he said, as he bared his teeth in a wolfish smile. He had the look of an animal about to attack its prey.

For a moment she didn't stir, then she burst out into loud, devilish laughter.

"That snotty little brat," she managed to stammer, between fits of laughter, pointing to me.

"Yes, your daughter."

"She's no daughter of mine," she said scornfully, looking at me with hatred in her eyes.

"Then who is she?" he asked in surprise.

"She's the daughter of my good-for-nothing husband. But of what use will she be to you? She knows nothing. If she was not so green, do you think I would keep her in here? I'm waiting for her to grow up a bit, and then, I'll send her on to the streets to earn her living… "

"Well, she can begin now, can't she?" he said, "That's exactly why I want her, because she knows nothing. If you let me have her, I'll give you this big bottle and ten more like it, and a bunch of dollars that you can spend as you fancy.

He approached the bottle to her mouth once again, and then pulled it away. She began to scream, beside herself,

"To Hell with you, American. Take her, take her. Only give me a drink, give me a drink…"

He gave her the bottle, but first, I saw him add a little white powder and shake it up well. She grasped the bottle and began drinking like mad. He waited for her to empty it.

Then, she lay motionless on the muddy floor. He pushed her with his foot and called her name. She gave no sign of having heard. She was dead to the world…in a coma. Now, I know that the white powder was a sleeping draft. He came near me and took me by the hand.

"Now you and I will have a drink together," he said.

"I don't want to," I stammered.

"What do you mean, you don't want to?" he shouted and glared at me, and I felt terrified as he put his hands to my throat, as if to strangle me.

He took another little bottle out of his pocket and made me drink. I drank because I was too frightened to refuse. He made me empty the bottle. My head began to spin, and my sight was blurred.

"Come here, near me, now I'm going to teach you a game that you'll like very much..."

I don't remember anything after that. But I remember those words, and I'll remember them till I die. They come back to me so often, so very often, and when they do, I must drink, drink to forget them. If I don't, I'll go mad.

That pain brought me round, out of that lethargy, for a moment. I began to swing my arms about......

"It's fun," someone whispered in my ears.

I began to scream. He put his hand over my mouth. Then he gagged me with a handkerchief that smelt of tobacco and of something else, which now I know was dope. I lay still, I felt myself falling into a deep, deep abyss, falling, falling...

Mr. District Attorney, you don't know what it means to feel yourself falling into an abyss, with no place to catch hold of, with no one to save you. You just know that you will crash to the bottom of the abyss, and you wait, but you never reach the bottom, you just float in mid-air, getting deeper and deeper...

I felt that my body was being torn to pieces as I floated in space. I heard voices and laughter. But I could see no light. A veil of darkness had descended over my eyes and over my mind. I felt that I was being buffeted about by icy winds, like a leaf in the fall.

I had no head, no arms, no legs. I could neither speak nor see. I felt nothing but that piercing pain burning into my flesh. I was trying to catch hold of something intangible as if it were real. I was lost. I was nothing. I was no longer alive. Yes, Mr. District Attorney I DIED that night, that cursed night. I was killed by two criminals that no law has punished...

That little girl was crucified that night. She was crucified like Christ. She died amid frightful pains, but she was never resurrected like Christ. There was nothing left of that little girl... A prostitute was born... That prostitute was I, Terezina…

When I regained consciousness, I was flooded with blood. He was lying next to me, fast asleep. She was trying to bring me round. When I opened my eyes, she began to threaten me that she would kill me if I told anybody about what had happened.

"I've got a terrible pain," I said, "that man did something to me."

"It's nothing," she said, " it had to happen one day. You'll get used to it. Now you'll earn more money than you did running errands and working for the greengrocer. Besides, that American is going to take you with him."

"Where's he going to take me to?"

"To a rich country, where you'll live like a queen. And mind you don't forget me, Terezina; you must always remember that you owe your good fortune to me, so you must send me money, because you're going to be rich…"

For ten days, or maybe more, I can't remember exactly, I had to stay in bed, as I could not walk. Then, one day, when I was just about able to stand on my feet, the American came again. He took me in his arms and the hideous pain was with me once more…

After that, I used to sleep with him regularly. He took me away from the hut. We went to live in a nice house with white walls and fine furniture. This went on for months. Then, my stepmother began to complain to the American that he didn't give her enough money; she kept on asking for more.

The American gave her some, but one night, he took me away. He had adopted me, he said, and now I was to call him DERRY.

He managed to get a passport for me and to bring me here to the U.S.A. as his daughter.

For two years, he consumed my body like a hungry wolf. I was then fourteen years old. During those two years, he forced me to make love with countless men; I never dared disobey him. I had no friends in this new country he had brought me to, and I was afraid he might turn me out if I did not do as he told me. That's why I slept with any men he brought round to the house.

Once, he brought a negro. I didn't want to sleep with him; I was scared of him, he was so very black. I'd never seen such a dark negro before. But when we were alone, he stroked my hair, and said, "Why did you come away from your own country, kid?"

"Derry brought me here," I said.

Then he stood up, and lifted me off the bed. He turned and spat on the floor, gave me some dollars to give Derry, and walked out of the room uttering the word 'Derry' with the greatest disgust.

That's how I learnt how to judge men by their feelings and not by the color of their skin. The negro could put many whites to shame. He taught me a good lesson.

But from that day, Derry did not touch me again. I was afraid he would turn me out... Then, I went to Mammy...

She was an elderly woman. She said she was fifty, but I would swear she was older than that. She used to wear bright-colored dresses, with low necklines, and her make-up was striking... She chose the girls from the lounge and sent them to the customers who had rang up asking for a girl. She took a liking to me, and it was clear that I was her favorite...

"How can you make a man love you, keep him near you, and make him your slave?" I asked her.

"I understand," she laughed, "there's a man you want to keep interested. But you mustn't use big, hollow words in our profession. Words such as love..... They are wasted. There is only bought love. The art of keeping a man's desire roused, that's what you should have said. In your country, in Greece, long ago, there were many famous whores who grew very rich just by knowing to perfection the art of love-making."

"Couldn't I become like one of them?" I asked.

"Yes, of course you can. Come and let me teach you some of their secrets."

She unbuttoned her robe, and began to throw off her undies, one by one. I watched with wide-open eyes.

"Come on," she cried. "What are you waiting for? Get undressed."

"But we are both women," I protested. "How can you teach me the love that men want?"

"Strip, and never you mind." she cried.

I began to undress; I could not understand how one woman could teach another how to make love to a man.

"Is it difficult?" I asked as I threw off my last bit of clothing.

"No, it's not at all difficult. Just stand up straight and let me admire you."

She looked me over as if I were an article of great value.

"Hum!" she said, "You're a peach, a real smasher. When you're a bit older, and have filled out a bit, you'll be worth a million dollars. But you're quite good now, you earn more than the other girls..."

She puffed at her cigar as she drew a sigh.

"You've got a beautiful body," she said, sighing again, "I was like that when I was young."

I didn't answer her. I was used to hearing old women say they had been beautiful in their youth. There never seemed to have been an ugly one!

"You could tempt a saint, Terezina," continued Mammy.

"Did the saints make love?" I asked in wonderment.

"I don't know if they made love, but I know that they had children. Now how a child can be born without its parents making love, is beyond me."

"I don't understand much about saints," I said.

"Neither do I, but if the saints really existed, let us hope they'll bless our new venture," she said.

"What venture?" I asked.

"Didn't you know that you are to deliver the dope to the various customers? You're the only girl the police don't suspect...yet."

"What's dope?" I asked.

"Haven't you seen all those chaps snoring in arm-chairs, every evening in the lounge?"

"Yes, I've seen them."

"Well, what do you think they're snoring for, because they are tired? They've had their fix. Very often, we've got the trouble of carrying them home."

"Who did that job before? I asked.

"Elena."

"Elena, my friend?"

"Yes! she answered drily, without looking at me.

"Well, why can't she carry on with the job?"

"Because she's washed-up. She's no good for the job any more, and tomorrow we're going to decide if we'll let her live."

"Are you going to kill her?" I asked in fear. "Are you going to kill her, like you killed Jenny?"

"We killed Jenny because she thought she was too clever. She wanted to give up her profession because she'd fallen in love with a foal who wanted to marry her, in spite of her past."

"But Elena didn't turn traitor," I protested. "She worked faithfully for you for years. Please, Mammy, don't let Derry kill her. She's my only friend, and I love her."

She looked at me while puffing at her disgusting cigar.

"If I let her live, will you do as you are told?" she asked.

"I promise you, Mammy, I'll do whatever you tell me, but don't let them kill Elena."

"Okay, Terry, you've won. I'll see what I can do."

"Oh, thank you, Mammy, I can't thank you enough..." I was delighted.

"I may be hard, but I'm just, Terry. That's why I'm still alive."

"I feel cold," I complained.

"Dress yourself, then."

"But aren't you going to teach me how to make love?"

"There's plenty of time for that. It can wait. Besides, there are sure to be others to give you some tips."

Then, she came and stood before me. She put her hand under my chin and lifted my face.

"To be honest, Terry," she said, "I would much rather you had nothing to do with our business, I'd rather you left this place. Unfortunately, both you and I are under this same roof. The roof that hides the sky from us and deprives us of fresh air, in any case, you're doomed to become a whore, you can't escape that fate now, it's too late. But listen to a piece of advice; it's not very righteous advice, but it's useful: try to have a bank account of your own, if you don't want to finish up like poor Elena…"

At that moment, the door opened, and Derry came in. Luckily, we had had time to get dressed.

"What are you doing here?" he asked coldly.

"I was telling her about the dope," said Mammy.

"Oh."

"And Terry is willing to do the job."

"Are you?" he asked as he turned towards me.

"Yes, I am," said without exactly knowing what was expected of me.

"And will you sleep with any man? Even with a black?"

"Yes, with any man, even with a black, but no one shall harm my friend Elena." I said.

"That's up to her," he said drily.

"She won't cause you any trouble, Derry."

"That's to be seen," he said. "Now, come along with me."

Before we left the room, I turned and looked at Mammy. I could read fear in her eyes. I had begun to understand two things, however. That at times I must keep my mouth shut tight, and that now I had got an ally.

A FOURTEEN-YEAR-OLD PROSTITUTE

At fourteen, I was a full-fledged prostitute. I made love with any man who came my way; all I cared about was my fee. I would take on anyone who paid me well.

Some of them liked to take me to their homes for two or three days. They paid Derry very well for my company.

It was Easter-time, Mr. District Attorney. I had to go and spend some days with an old man in a villa not far from New York. Derry drove me there in his car. A white Mercedes. He handed me over to the old man, who must have been about sixty. Before leaving, Derry looked at me fiercely and said, "Don't make a fuss, whatever he does to you. If I find out that you've crossed him, I'll kill you. You must do everything to please the old bloke, got me?"

"Yes, Derry, I'll do my best to please him," I said, trembling with fear.

"Here she is, Professor, I'm sure you'll spend a very pleasant time with Terry."

"I hope so," said the old man, as he ogled me lustfully.

Derry left. The old man put his arm round my shoulders and we went inside the villa. At once, he bolted the door.

The day after Easter I heard the church bells ringing over the radio. The old man and I were lying in bed. Suddenly, I asked him, "Why did they crucify Christ, Professor?"

"This is hardly the time for such a question," he said. "Come on, give me a kiss."

"Was it because he couldn't get together the thirty pieces of silver to pay Judas? And that made Judas get it from the Jews? I've heard say that all the story about Christ was because of thirty pieces of silver that Judas needed."

"I daresay Christ was broke," said the Professor.

"But as he was God, with so much power, why did he let himself get caught, and tortured, and then crucified? Why didn't he escape to Heaven?"

"Because he was a fool," said the Professor calmly. "But I am not a fool to let you lie here talking and talking, when I have to pay your Derry a stiff fee for your services. I want to kiss you."

He glued his lips to mine, and so I never got to the bottom of Christ's story, because once more, I was being crucified.

So you see, Mr. District Attorney, why I have never been able to solve that mystery.

One day, I asked the Professor to let me go for a walk outside the villa, which was surrounded by beautiful, green, open country.

He let me go, because he had to do some shopping in town. As soon as he drove off, I locked the villa, put the key in my pocket and set out.

I hadn't seen such green fields for years. I got carried away by the beauty around me. I gazed in admiration at everything, forgetting myself and getting farther and farther away from the villa.

When I die, I should like it to be in such a place as that, with the birds singing in the branches, the golden sunshine overhead, the bright, green grass and the wild flowers a multi-colored carpet to lie on. I wonder who this God was who had made such wonderful things, Whoever he was and wherever He might be, I wanted to beg him to let me die in a place like that. Only then would I be happy. I walked through a little wood and came to a clearing where some sheep were grazing. I joyfully ran towards the flock.

It was so pleasant there, the grass smelt so sweet, the sky was a deep blue. I ran among the sheep like a child playing a new game. As a child, I had never had the chance to play... But the sheep took fright and scattered in all directions, their little bells tinkling…

Surely, paradise must be something like that... I caught sight of a little lamb. I tried to catch it, but it ran off. I went after it, laughing as I saw it stop, look at me, and then gambol off again, shaking its little tail. It fooled me several times; it let me get near it, and just as I put out my hand to touch it, it would slyly skip away. I fell full-length on the grass once or twice in my endeavor to catch it.

"Come here, little lamb," I said. "I won't do you any harm, I only want to pet you, and then you can go back to your mother, now stop teasing me…"

But it continued its antics, frisking about on the grass, and never letting me get too near it. I sat down on the grass, disappointed and exhausted.

"You're a nasty, wicked, heartless little lamb," I said, "just like Derry."

"It's neither wicked nor heartless, but just scared."

I turned to see who had spoken. I immediately realized that it was the shepherd. He was holding a little lamb in his arms and was giving it to me.

"They don't know you; that's why they won't come near you.

Here, take this one, but hold it gently. I'm going to get the flock together again. They scattered when you began chasing them. Hold the lamb, and if it kicks, mind you don't let it go. I'll be back soon."

He left his shoulder-bag near me, picked up his crock, and ran towards the trees.

I was left nursing the lamb. I had never held anything so lovable in my arms before. I bent and whispered in its ear, "I love you little lamb, I swear I do, I've never loved any other creature in my life…What, don't you believe me?" I asked as I saw its eyes fixed upon me. "I love you. I loved the mice in the hut, because they kept me warm in winter, but they've forgotten me by now. Don't think I love Derry, because I don't. I'm afraid of him, that's all. I'm scared of him, as you are scared of the wolf. But you've got that young shepherd to protect you from the wolf. He may be wearing dirty old clothes, your shepherd, but he's tall and handsome. Derry wears clean, new clothes, but he's a filthy pimp. Besides, little lamb, you've got a faithful sheep-dog, too. But I have neither dog nor shepherd."

The hearty laugh of the shepherd, who had returned without my hearing him, put an end to my talk with the lamb.

"You're not a lamb to need the protection of a shepherd or of a dog, you're a young girl, or rather I should say, a little girl. Come and sit here by me."

"I'm a big girl," I said, straightening up and letting the lamb run away.

"Ha, ha, ha," he laughed louder than ever, "How old are you?"

"I'm fourteen," I said.

"Then you're right, you are really a big girl! What's your name?" he asked.

"Terry," I said.

"Terry? What name is that?" he asked.

"Terezina," I answered.

"Ah," he said, "What's brought you here, Terezina?"

"I was just wandering about the countryside, on this lovely soft grass. Your lambs are little darlings."

"Do you live nearby, Terezina? I've never seen you round about here before."

"I live at the villa at the edge of the forest."

"With the old man?"

"Yes, with the old man."

"Is he a relative of yours?"

I looked him in the eyes and said mockingly, "Don't ask too many questions. Tell me about yourself. How do you like living in the country?"

"I like it fine. I love nature, and I love my flock."

"Have you got a girlfriend?" I asked point blank.

"No," he answered calmly, looking at me in surprise.

"Do you want me to be your girlfriend?"

"To be my girlfriend!"

"Yes, we'll make love, we'll run about on the grass, we'll play hide-and-seek in the wood, and we'll chase the sheep."

"But you've got to go back to the villa in a while, Terezina, and then to town."

"I'll go back, but I'll often come and see you, very often."

He looked at me. "You're beautiful, Terezina, but you are far too young for such things."

"I've been told that many times before."

"Why do you want to make love with me, Terezina?"

"Because I make love with all the men that come my way," I answered frankly.

"Aren't you afraid of strange men?"

"No, why should I? What else can they do to me besides make love?"

"Is that what you do with the old man?"

"Yes, with the old man, too," I answered as I looked away.

"Go away!" he said as he jumped to his feet.

"Why?" I asked him, "Aren't you a man? Don't you want to make love with a beautiful woman?"

"You're not a woman, you're a child. Can't you understand that?"

"I'm a woman," I cried stubbornly. "A loose woman."

He didn't wait to hear any more. He seized me in his arms and tumbled me in the soft grass. He fondled me and kissed me with such ardor, passion, and tenderness that I was taken by surprise.

For two years, I had been a common little whore. I had slept with a great variety of men. Most of them were far from normal in their love-making. But this shepherd was so manly, so natural, so normal…

The trees formed a bower over our heads, the almond trees and the cherry trees were white with blossoms. How I would have loved to have placed a wreath of white flowers on my head. But the idea only passed fleetingly through my mind at the moment the shepherd and I were one…

The little lamb looked at us in a strange way, then it ran bleating to its mother.

We lay on the grass watching the little clouds sail through the sky…

"Do you believe in God?" I asked him.

"I do," he answered as he turned towards me.

"What is God?"

"I can't tell you, Terezina, but I believe in Him."

"I say God is the creation of man's imagination." I felt proud that I had found someone to talk to on the subject that preoccupied me so much.

"I don't think man's imagination is strong enough to create a God," he said.

"Why not?"

"Because God is the Universe. God created man. How can man be equal to Him?"

"Anyhow, men don't love Him. When I asked the Professor the other day about Christ, he told me that He was a fool."

"Has he got a lot of books?"

"His house is full of them."

"Well, he must have read so many that he's got all muddled up."

"I suppose that's it." I admitted, "Derry says that whoever reads the nonsense written in books is a bloody idiot."

"Who is Derry? You told me you had no folks of your own."

"That's true, I've no parents, but I've got a Derry."

"I don't get you, Terezina."

"It's hard to explain. You can't understand this, as I can't understand about God, and about Christ. He had the power to escape to Heaven, instead of letting Himself be crucified, but He didn't. Was He such a fool? Do you think the Professor is right?"

"That's a long and complicated story. Most people can't make sense of it, but they make the sign of the cross like idiots... shall we go for a run?"

"Yes, let's," I said.

"If I catch you, we'll make love again."

We ran about for a long time. Then, I went and fell into his arms. He laid me down on the grass, and this time our love-making was more subdued.

He wanted to get up, but I wouldn't let him. I wanted to feel his body near mine. To smell the sweetness of his breath, and to sense his joy as I offered him my lips.

"How old are you?" I asked him.

"Twenty."

"Have you made love with other girls?"

"Two or three times. But not one was so beautiful and so sweet as you, Terezina. You haven't even asked me my name."

"Please don't tell me your name. I've heard so many men's names, that I'm afraid I might get them mixed up with yours. I want to know you as my shepherd, handsome, red-haired, poorly dressed, but a real gentleman."

"You are sweet, Terezina, sweet and adorable, I can't have my fill of you."

"No man ever has his fill of me," I said proudly.

"Why do you make love with so many men, Terezina?"

"They pay me, that's why."

"But I didn't pay you."

"I won't take money from you, I'm your girlfriend."

"Terezina, give up that way of living, and come and live here with me."

"I can't," I said seriously.

"Why not?"

"Derry would never let me. He makes a lot of money by trading my body, and if I ever go against his wishes, he beats me badly."

"You shouldn't put up with that, it's unfair."

"Derry doesn't know the meaning of that word. He is always in the right....."

"Why don't you run away?"

"He'll track me down, wherever I go."

"I'll hide you here on the mountain."

"He'll find us, then he'll kill you, and I don't want you to come to any harm, because I've been very happy here with you."

"Will you come back often, Terezina?"

"I'll come, but not very often. Later on, when I've got a car of my own. I'll come nearly every day. Now I must go back to the villa before the old man returns, if he gets back and I'm not there, he'll ring up Derry, and then there will be trouble."

The old man was back. And soon as he saw me he started shouting, "Where have you been all day? I've been looking everywhere for you. I rang up Derry to ask if you'd gone back home."

"Why did you do that?" I whined, "You know what Derry's like. He'll be mad with me."

"Alright, alright, don't fret, I'll ring him back and say you're here."

When the old man came upstairs, he found me lying on the bed.

"I can't be angry with you," he said, "You've such a lovely body, you drive me crazy."

I was in no mood to respond to the old man's lovemaking that night, but he got the better of my indifference with his harsh words, "I pay you, you depraved creature, I pay you."

I slept very badly that night, because I realized that I would never be able to make love with one man, ever...

I stayed with the old professor two more days. But he would not let me outside the villa, so I had no opportunity of meeting the shepherd again...

When Derry came to fetch me, he was kinder and more attentive than ever before. "This time, you were a credit to me, Terry. The old man was very pleased with you, so pleased that he has asked me to take you to him again. And there was no haggling about money. He paid well and without a murmur. Next time, we'll make him give us more, won't we, Terry?!"

"That will be fine."

"I missed you these days. And some other gentlemen missed you too, many of them."

"Do you want me, Derry?"

"You know I can't do without you. You're my right hand. Now you'll have the other job too, you are to deliver the dope to the customers at their homes."

"How will I do that?"

"You'll take the dope to them hidden in the heels of your shoes, or in your hair."

"What's dope, Derry?" I asked. "I've heard Mammy say that it kills people."

"What do we care if it kills them or not? All we care about is our business."

"And how will I get to the customers' homes?"

"In a few days' time, you'll have your driving license."

"But I can hardly drive, and besides, I'm too young to get a license."

"Alky will teach you to drive. As to how you'll get your license, that's my affair."

"I don't want Alky near me; he's a brute, he tortures the girls."

Alky was one of Derry's gorillas. He was the one who tortured the girls to make them obey Derry's orders.

"You are not for Alky, I need you."

"It's not right, Derry, to give people stuff that kills them."

"Don't talk nonsense, Terry. We can't give it to them by force, they come begging for it."

"If the police should find out?" I tried to scare him. But Derry was afraid of no one, not even of the Devil, perhaps because he was one with the Devil.....

"That's one of the reasons why you must take over now. Elena must leave off, the cops have got wise to her, and if she falls into their hands, they'll soon make her spill the beans, the state she's in now. Besides, Elena is past her prime now, and she's no more use to us."

"How old is Elena?"

"I think she's about twenty-three."

"And you call that past her prime?"

"For our job, she's far too old.

"What work can she do now then?"

"That's her headache. Drink was her downfall. I used to tell her so, but she'd take no notice. She fell in love with a bloke, and because he left her in the lurch, she took to drink, and now she's messed up our business."

"How's she going to live?"

"That's no concern of mine."

"Shall we give her some money, Derry? She's been working for you since she was fifteen... Others have worked..."

"I know what you're going to say, but just you listen to me. Other girls worked for us, they were even younger than Elena when they began, but we sent them packing without even a 'thank you'. Bear that in mind. In our world, there is no room for mercy. Sentiment is dead. We kept Elena on a bit longer because she used to push the dope. Now that the police have got wind of it, she's got to stop."

"And what if Elena won't leave?"

"She'll never dare stand up to me, as no one has ever dared, up to this minute."

"Derry, hadn't we better let Elena come to the lounge, even if the customers will have none of her? At least she'll be able to get a free drink there. Elena was always such a kind girl. Do you remember how she looked after me when I was ill?

"No, I won't have any beggars in the lounge. She must never set foot in there again. She'll have a cop on her tail, and then we'll have to bump him off. That will mean more trouble. She should be thankful we've let her live, what more does she want?"

I made no further attempt to plead Elena's cause. But I decided to help her on the quiet, without Derry and his mob finding out.

"Okay," I said indifferently, "It's no affair of mine how Elena lives. Only don't kill her, because it will make me very sad."

He turned and looked at me with that sly, sneaky look in his eyes.

"Alright, we'll let her live a few more days for your sake."

I turned my face away, because I didn't want him to see the sadness in my eyes. Gee, how I hated him!

A week later, I had a car of my own. A little red Fiat. It became my accomplice in crime. In it, I drove to our customers' homes, delivering the 'white death', dope...

One afternoon, I finished early, so I could spare an hour or two with the shepherd. He showed no joy at seeing me.

"How many men have you slept with lately? You must have been very busy. Of course you had no time to come here."

"Don't be silly," I said, "I've slept with no end of men. If I met them in the street, I wouldn't recognize them, but that doesn't mean I've forgotten you."

"You're a whore," he spat out with contempt. And at that Moment, I felt as if he had rubbed my face in the mud.

"I had told you that at the very beginning. You must admit feet and looked at me, his eyes searching my face.

"Why don't you go and ask help from the police?"

"That's out of the question. If I did that, Derry would kill me at once."

"But why?"

"Don't ask why, I'll explain another time. I can't tell you anything now. There's no time, Please tell me, will you hide my friend here?"

He thought for a while.

"Bring her," he said, "I'll do what I can to help save her.

I'm sorry I spoke to you like that, Terezina, I see you're in trouble. But please tell me what's up."

A happy smile lit my face. A smile straight from my heart. I stood on tiptoes and kissed him on the forehead.

"Thank you, I'll bring her now, then I'll explain everything."

I ran down to the road, where I had left my car. I was full of joy, but I didn't know that two malicious eyes were watching me.

MY FRIEND ELENA

Unconsciously, and for the first time in my life, I called upon God. "God, if you exist, whoever you are, wherever you are, why did you do this?"

Those were my first words when I saw Elena and the state she was in. I had gone to her hotel to fetch her away. A low- class hotel in the heart of New York, frequented by Blacks and by loose women who sold themselves to the scum of the earth...

Surely that wasn't Elena. The Elena I knew and loved, my one and only friend. This girl looked twice her age, she was beyond recognition. She was holding a bottle, and she was drinking, drinking... without a pause, without a halt.

"Why have you come? she stammered, when she took the bottle out of her mouth. "You should not have come. If Derry finds out, you'll be in trouble...

"Shit on Derry's bloody face," I said as I knelt beside her.

"I don't care, I want to help save you, because you know I love you, Elena."

"I know you love me, Terry. But I don't think you love only me."

"Once, I had another love," I said bitterly, "now, I love only you."

"Whom did you love?" she asked me, staring at me with her drunken eyes.

I looked at her and my heart sank. I knew she expected me to say that I had loved a handsome youth, or one of my wealthy customers. I did not answer her at once, let her have her illusions. Then, I said.

"I once loved a little animal, a kitten. When I felt cold in winter, it used to sleep at my feet and keep them warm. When there was ice in my heart, I used to take it in my arms, for warmth and comfort. But when I was taken away by Derry, and brought here to sell my body, the kitten was left all alone and desolate. But, perhaps, less so than I...."

She looked at me strangely. "Haven't you ever loved a human?"

"I never loved, because I was never loved".

"You're right" she said. "It's hard for a whore to be loved. But animals love better than humans, because they don't mind if you are a whore."

"Yes, animals love better than humans," I said as I went to draw the curtains.

"Terry, you know, I loved - I loved and that's why I'm going to die." She lifted the bottle she was holding and drank deeply.

"They say that love is…"

"Wonderful," she interrupted, laughing sarcastically. "It's nothing. All it does is make you suffer. And I the fool loved.

I loved him so much, that I brought about my own ruin. When I was just a whore, I had my dignity. Now I've lost it. Imagine, he told me one day he couldn't go on living with a whore, and he left me…" She put the whisky bottle to her mouth and swallowed in great gulps. Then, she passed the bottle to me. I drank some, too, to buck myself up. I knew what I had planned to do was very dangerous, that Derry would never forgive me. If he caught me, I was lost, because the gang had condemned Elena to death.

She took the bottle from my hand and began talking in an absent-minded way, "The night he left me, I felt lost. I felt I was choking. I couldn't breathe. I couldn't lift that heavy weight off my chest. The weight that was loneliness. I wanted someone to pull away that hand with cruel, sharp nails that was squeezing my heart.

I felt the blood drain from my body, drop by drop. I thought I heard the drops falling onto the carpet, in the quiet of the night, and they sounded like the slow tread of the dead.

I could see that hand coming out of my chest, clasping my heart, and coming near my throat. My cry of fear was so loud that the bird flew screeching from its cage. It flew madly round the room, and then came back to perch on the top of its cage... It looked around in fright...

As I was kneeling on the carpet, I lifted my eyes and looked at the bird. Through my blurred vision, I could see whole flocks of crows devouring carrion without appeasing their hunger. Do you know anything about crows? When the carrion isn't enough to satisfy them, they devour one another. Then, the bird got smaller and smaller. And we were alone in the room, the bird and I."

Mr. District Attorney, although three years have passed since then, I can hear Elena's voice in my ears at this very moment.

"Only birds are good, Terezina. Only birds are good."

"Yes, only birds are good," I said as I stroked her untidy hair.

Elena looked at me and passed me the bottle again. The booze burnt my inside, but it gave me new courage.

'That morning I got up and opened the window wide," continued Elena. "The icy cold wind blew the curtains about like the sails of a wrecked ship.

'Go away,' I cried to the bird... 'Go'... But it would not move. It shrunk into its feather and hopped back into its cage.

"You are right," I said. "Where can you go? There's frost outside, but there's frost even inside - for me..."

As I turned to close the window, I saw the houses across the street with their lighted windows. There were thousands of lights everywhere, in the streets, in the houses, lights of all colors—some big, some small, and they all mocked me. Those lighted windows were like the mouths of the damned.

I slammed the window shut as I dashed for a drink of whisky. I drained a glassful in one draught, then, I lay on the carpet and went on drinking glass after glass. I felt I was in paradise. Then, I got up and began smashing everything within reach...

I yelled and screamed and broke everything in the room. Nothing was left whole, then, I opened the door and ran barefoot into the street."

"What made you go into the street, Elena, dear?" I asked, my voice trembling with emotion.

"I was looking for a man. Any man. A beggar. A cripple. A thief. A drunk, a blackmailer, a sadist, a criminal. Any one, just a man. To get drunk with him, to make love with him, to share my loneliness with him. I didn't care what his color was—black, white, yellow. I wanted a man's company. I could not be alone. But I couldn't find anyone. The roads were deserted. Deep and dreary. It was raining by the cold wind. It was Hell, and I was one of the damned.

I went up to my room in tears. I dropped to and lay on the carpet, motionless, my eyes fixed on the ceiling. I could hear steps in the corridor of the hotel. I could hear the rain. I could hear the death rattle of my broken heart."

Elena lifted the bottle and drank with frenzy. Exhausted, she dropped to her knees, as if to beg the past to leave her in peace. The past had returned once again, and this time, drink could not send it away. Her face was waxen, she looked half-dead. Her lips were white, and her gaze was vacant.

"A few days ago, my memories returned from the grave. They had been to meet my lost dreams. They had gone to meet all those people I had killed with the dope your Derry made me give them…"

I knelt next to her. I took her in my arms.

"Where do the dead live, Elena? We both have to beg their forgiveness."

"They say they live in Heaven, but the surest is that they live under the ground, where we put them. Do you know, Terry, I'm going away," she said all of a sudden.

"Where are you going to?" I asked anxiously.

"Where the birds go when they are beaten by the lashing rain. I'll do the same, I'll go to a warm country. I'm so very cold here."

"Wherever you go now, my dear Elena, there will be nothing but rain and snow for you. No country will be as warm as the one you were born and reared in. Here, at least you know a few people who will say a kind word to you, but if you go to an unknown country…"

"The birds are hunted by the hunters wherever they go. But they fly to other countries. Perhaps, they go away in order to forget, too…" I nodded my head. Elena was right.

"Terry, humans are ungrateful creatures. They are never satisfied with what God has given them; they never have enough.

They always take whatever they can from others. People are cruel, Terry. As long as they live, they never have enough, but when they die, a grave is more than enough. Only the birds are good. They fly in the sky, and the sky is pure, even when it's covered with clouds…"

"You are right, Elena, only birds are good." She turned her back on me and began drinking again, trying to calm her shattered nerves, to sate her wrath, her fear of the death that awaited her. She wanted to scream and to shriek. But nothing would come of that. When night fell, she knew it would be much worse. The quiet and the darkness would become an open grave, and she a ghost haunting it. Her despair was increasing. She was cold, and she hugged herself to keep warm. But to no avail. Or she would look at the door, and her heart would beat faster and faster, her white lips trembled, and her teeth chattered for fear…

Lips and teeth were one like the white wound of a leper, her tongue showed white, too… She held her breath when she heard steps in the corridor, or she would say, "They're coming to kill me, Terry. Go away, go away, save yourself. Terry, I love you, my little one, and I don't want them to kill you." I put my arms around her.

"Don't be afraid, Elena," I comforted her. "They won't kill you.

They know I love you and that if they do you any harm, I'll kill them."

"How many of them can you kill, Terry, dear? They are so many scattered all over the place, like wolves."

She fell onto the bed, her body shaken by sobs. Derry and his gang were driving her out of her mind by threatening her with death every day, then letting her live. In this way, they increased her fear and panic to such a point that she no longer had the power to refuse them anything.

I used to be able to comfort her. That evening, however, I was powerless. I knew that her fate had been sealed by those killers—Derry's gang. Elena was of no use to them any longer, so she had to die. She was dangerous goods now...

That evening, when work was over, they were going to kill her. YOU MUST NOT be kind in this life, Mr. District Attorney. When you are kind, you are treated with ingratitude and sadism.

"Elena," I said. "Try and understand what I'm going to tell you, however tipsy you may be. I know you'll understand if you try. I've come to take you away, to save you from the death they are threatening you with. Tonight, after midnight, they've decided to kill you. Mammy told me so. I've come to take you away, now. I'm going to take you to a place where Derry will never find you. Do you understand, Elena?"

Her eyes were fixed on mine, full of anguish and despair.

"Where are you going to take me? To which of your lovers? Derry knows them all, none will want to get mixed up with him," her voice was very weak.

I could barely catch her faint words. She hadn't the strength to speak any louder. There were dark shadows under her eyes, the result of long bouts of drinking. Her pupils could only just be seen. Her nose was red from crying the tears that ran from her tired eyes, like early morning dew-drops on a withered leaf.

"No, we are not going to any blackguardly friend of Derry's," I said.

"I'll take you far away from all that filth, where there is no sign of Derry and his gang. Come on, get up, try to stand on your feet. Help me."

"If I disappear, Derry will kill you. He'll guess that you helped me—"

"Shit on him," I said. "He won't do anything to me."

Her eyes were glued on my face, as if she were trying to read my thoughts. I had great difficulty in concealing my fear, but worst of all was hiding the nausea her foul breath caused me. Foul from drink and hunger. As she approached her face to mine, the stench was terrible, as if her inside was already dead.

"They're going to kill me, Terry. They've made up their minds at last. I'm going to die. There's no getting away from them this time".

"You know them, Elena. You've seen them kill, you know them better than I do. You've seen what they've done to others. Now, your turn has come. Tomorrow, it will be mine... So, get up, Elena, let's get out of here."

She leant against me, she almost hurting herself onto me. Her legs could hardly hold her. She was half-paralyzed by terror and booze, and her body was a dead weight. I helped her out on her overcoat, and it was a job getting her to the elevator.

When we got to the garage where I had parked my car, I was bathed in sweat...

I put her on the seat next to me and covered her with my coat. She had begun to tremble. I drove off cautiously, not to draw anyone's attention.

When I was out of New York, I pressed my foot on the accelerator and felt a feeling of elation.

But Mr. District Attorney, there is no escaping Satan's will.

When you are with SATAN…

RUTHLESS KILLERS

I reached my destination. I helped Elena out of the car, then took her by the hand. I led her to where I was to meet the shepherd. I wondered why my young friend wasn't there to meet us, but not for a moment did I suspect what had happened.

How could I imagine that Derry and his gang had forestalled me, here in this lonely spot? I thought that the shepherd had wandered away with his flock, as I was rather late in coming...

"Where are you, my friend? I called.

But I got no answer. My voice echoed through the wood. I left Elena and ran towards the trees.

"Friend, where are you?"

Still no answer. I looked to right and left, with a dull foreboding this time. The darkness was denser among the trees. I tried to make out a shadow I saw moving about. Then, I saw one of Derry's bullies emerging from behind the trees. My first thought was for Elena.

"Elena," I cried with all the strength of my lungs. "Run away as fast as you can, take the car and drive off. They'll kill you. Someone has betrayed us, Elena."

I ran to her help. I knew she was still too drunk to understand me. But Elena had understood and had begun to run, stumbling and swaying towards the car. Three of Derry's most blood-thirsty villains were at her heels.

My heart was pounding, fit to burst. All I could do was scream at the top of my voice, "Run, Elena, run."

But her legs were weak, and although fear and panic lent her wings, the effects of the drink hindered her progress.

They soon caught up with her. They rushed upon her with fury. They pulled her by the legs towards me. I fell upon them like a tigress, and I tore at them with my nails. But they were three, and I was one. They left her at my feet. Her face was covered with blood, and blood was pouring on to the ground from the wounds caused by their kicks and blows, and by the thorns that had tom her flesh as they had dragged her along the ground. Her arms were outspread like a bird's broken wings.

I took her in my arms and tried to wipe the blood from her face. She slowly opened her eyes and fixed her gaze on me with surprise and misgiving. Two blood-shot eyes.

"You, too, wanted to kill me, Terry. That's way you brought me here."

I shuddered.

"No, no, Elena, Don't say that, I didn't want to kill you. I wanted to help you. I don't know how they got here. Forgive me, Elena, I wanted to save you. Say you believe me."

"I don't believe you, Terry. You, too, wanted to kill me. You're rotten through and through, Terry."

She didn't speak again, those were her last words...

"Enough of this comedy." It was Derry's voice. "Leave off weeping, it's bad for the health, and red swollen eyes are pad for trade. Think of your customers, you've got to look seductive. Take her away and finish her off like that other fellow..."

I lifted my eyes. Two eyes full of horror and revenge, two blood-shot eyes filled with hatred and rage. I fixed them on Derry and spoke with loathing and disgust.

"You are a fiend, Derry. A brute in human form. You are one of God's biggest mistakes, and I'll never forgive Him for that mistake. If you touch Elena, I'll kill you."

In answer, he gave me a hard kick in the stomach that sent me reeling. Elena slipped from my arms. Then, two arms seized her like two starving beasts. Two others seized me.

"You watch now, and you'll learn that you are no match for me," Derry hissed in my ear. "You'll die the way your friend is going to die now if you continue doing whatever comes into your head. All you whores are the same. See how Elena is going to die and blame yourself. You helped us in our plans.

We didn't know how to get rid of her lousy carcass. How it's easy. Hurry up Alky, get on with the job."

I saw Alky lay Elena on the ground face downwards. Then, he knelt on her neck, took hold of her head, and yanked it backwards. Her face went blue, her eyes wide-open and staring were blood red. A dull, rattling sound, a few jerks, as if she were trying to shake off the man who was torturing her, a last quiver of her feet, and she was still. The beast that had been kneeling on her got up.

"Now what shall I do with them, boss?" he asked Derry, shaking the dust off his hands.

I had not stirred all time. I was petrified with fear. Fear was everywhere. An unnatural, eerie fear.

I looked at Elena's dead body. I could barely hear what they were saying.

"What shall we do with them?" echoed Derry, still smoking his cigar, and calmly standing with one hand in his pocket, as if he were a director giving orders.

"But that's very simple, Alky. We were lucky that the old professor has the habit of gazing round the countryside through his field glasses.

He saw our little Terry meet that wretched shepherd and like a good friend, he put us wise..... So the shepherd decided to die, taking his beloved with him, because he couldn't bear to share her with others. Before you throw them on the railway lines, see that you write a decent little note... Because when our friends the cops find their mangled bodies on the railway lines, they must feel sorry for their misfortune, and after they put them under the sod, we'll be left in peace."

"Okay, Boss."

My eyes were motionless in their sockets. I was turned to stone. And when I saw them drag the dead body of the young shepherd towards poor Elena, then, my hatred for those rotten swine became an abyss, a bottomless pit...

Who had betrayed me? Was it the old professor? Derry, himself, had said so. Our only customer in these parts. So, my revenge would start from him. Derry's disagreeable voice recalled me to reality.

"You haven't asked why we killed your boyfriend?"

"Why should I ask about something I already know?" I said with disdain. "But you must know something. From this day, you've lost me forever, and if you dare, kill me too. The cops know I'm your daughter, and if I'm missing, the first person they'll begin to question will be you, Derry, and even if you go into the deepest mourning, you will not be believed."

Two cruel shadows danced in his eyes.

"Of course you know, Terry, that you'll never be able to get out of my grasp. You'll always be under my roof, you must become a real prostitute, body and soul. I'll give you a good example today. I want you to remember that your soul must be a vile as your body—that's how our work will get on well...

"I'm not afraid of you, Derry," I answered with courage and sarcasm. "I'm not at all afraid of you. What can you do to me? Beat me, ill-treat me. I don't care. You bought my body from my stepmother for a bottle of whisky. But my soul is mine. You'll never get it. You're beaten! And from now on, I'm the winner. You'll put up with me without being able to get rid of me. I told you not to touch Elena. You wouldn't listen. You not only killed Elena, but you killed the shepherd as well; he had done you no harm. Now you're to going to pay, continually. You'll pray day and night to find a way of getting rid of me. But I'll look after my health, just for your sake. Because one day, I'm going to kill you, Derry, with my own hands. You must never forget that. You must remember that whatever misfortune comes your way, I'll protect you just to have the chance of killing you myself. Be sure I'm going to kill you – you bloody pimp, you murderer…"

He couldn't hold back his rage. He flew at me with kicks and swearwords.

"I'll make you eat your words, you harlot, I'll make you swallow what you've said."

I didn't utter a cry of pain. And when he ordered his thugs to have their fill of me, and one by one they sated their sexual desires, I did not stir. I lay motionless, as if dead, and I submitted to the punishment he had imposed on me without the slightest reaction. I submitted to rape as a revenge on him.

I could stand on my feet when they let me be. They had left me stark naked. My clothes were in rags. My body was bruised - bloody in places. My lips, although disfigured by pain, wore a twisted smile.

"I told you, Derry. You had taught my body to put up with my pig and any brute like you."

I didn't have time to finish my sentence. A hard kick in the stomach made me spit blood and fall on the grass in a dead faint.

I felt them pushing me aside with their feet. Then I was caught and dragged along. I was being taken away. I felt at that moment that I was Elena.

DARK DAYS IN MY LIFE

I'll never be able to say for sure, Mr. District Attorney, how many days I lay, eyes shut and body motionless, after I was raped. The only thing I felt was a hand on my head and a women's voice swearing and cursing in anger, "The swine. The bloody murderer. The brutes."

It was Mammy who was nursing me back to health, helping me to get over the shock, and caring for my injuries of that day..... Mammy did her utmost to get me on my feet again, and when she finally succeeded, she was ever so proud.

"Listen to me, Terry," she said. "Don't make Derry too mad." She chewed on her cigar, then spat. "He'll kill you," she went on, "and I don't want you to come to any harm. I love you, as you loved Elena."

"How do you know how I loved Elena?" I asked in a hard voice.

"All you know is hiring out girls and smoking cigars."

She went on chewing and spitting. Then, she sat herself down cross-legged on the floor at my side.

"I suppose you're right, Terry, to speak to me like that, but it's only by doing Derry's bidding that I stay alive. Otherwise, I would have the same fate as Elena. As for Elena, I know that you were very fond of her. While you were ill, you were raving about her, and blaming yourself for her death. No, Terry that's not true. Elena knew you loved her and that you wanted to save her. Her last words were said in her confusion, in the death-panic that swept through her."

She stopped talking and rested her back against the wall. Then, she looked at me with a tired expression, as if talking had exhausted her.

Now, I was seeing her under another light. This short, fat, ugly, old woman still had a spark of humanity left in her, in spite of the years she had spent in depravity and immorality.

"I was once twenty years old, Terry. I was very much in demand, and I was highly paid for my services, as you are now... But time went by. When one is young, one is avid for pleasure, and too foolish to realize that a time will come when the abuses of loose living will take their toll. When I saw that my face and my figure were losing their youthfulness, I began to get desperate. I spent fabulous sums on beauty treatments to try and keep my good looks. Then, I realized that I was fighting a losing battle against time, so I began to seek comfort in drugs, trying to forget my plight in an induced, artificial sleep. The last penny of my meagre takings went to Derry, who supplied me with dope, and when I had nothing left, I resorted to begging. That was no good, either. Then, I turned to crime.

She drew up her legs with the swollen veins, and crouched, as if afraid of invisible shadows.

"Look at my hands, Terry. They are gnarled, but well-kept. Look at these well-varnished nails—their roots have been watered with human blood. I became Derry's most valuable helper. I have killed, and I still kill at his bidding, for my dose of dope... That is my wage since that fateful night. The night I stabbed a man in the back. He had come to Derry to get his charge — his dose of dope — but he had no money to pay for it, so Derry told him to scram... The fellow was desperate in his craving, so he lunged at Derry, but I was tooquick for him, plunged a knife in his back, and he was ripe for the lilies. That evening, Derry took me on to work in his den. A plate of food, my dose of dope, and as much booze as I could drink at the bar... That was my wage. My payment for bumping off anyone Derry lost interest in, or considered undesirable..."

She sensed my disgust, and said,

"Don't look at me like that. I know how you feel. You loathe me more than you loathe Derry."

I didn't answer her. I let her go on talking. I don't know why I let her go on, why I listened to her. Did she disgust me? Yes.... Did I hate her, though? No, I didn't. There was an excuse for her downfall. For her ruined life. An excuse that YOU, Mr. District Attorney, and your jurymen, would not take seriously. But I know that her excuse is genuine, indeed. I've been brought up in the underworld and can tell you that she was fully justified. Her excuse was OLD AGE.

Old age is a living death in the underworld. You are thought to be washed-up and dangerous, and your fate is decided over a game of cards and a glass of liquor...

The laws of our union are hard and merciless. Whoever can no longer be of service in our lounge has to die. Either young or old...

Every day, a name was ruled off the list of the villainous gang. All who were wounded in brawls with the police, in hold- ups or burglaries and were unable to make a getaway, had to be bumped off by their comrades, to keep them from blabbing when caught by the police. Dead men tell no tales...

Mammy asked for a light. I passed her my gold lighter with my initials on it, and she lit a second cigar. As she puffed at it, the smoke half-hid her painted face. She looked older and uglier than ever. She shifted into a more comfortable position.

"Terry, I know that advice from a woman like me is a bit of irony.

You might even think it's mockery. But I don't care; I just want you to listen to me. A whore can advise another whore about the ins and outs of her profession. Especially when she has priority, as in my case. You can't escape from the life you are leading now, nor from the claws of the vampire, Derry. Live the life of a whore, but live your own life.

You must become a super-whore. But only for yourself. But, Terry, keep away from narcotics, far from snow, hashish, marijuana.

Keep off all those poisons. You can be a pusher, sell them to spooks, but never get caught yourself. If you do, you'll turn into the ghost of your former self. Learn from an old harlot who has spent her life in dens of crime that the more a thing costs, the more ruinous it is.

"And what about Derry?" I asked.

"Drop him. He can't ham you, if he could, you would be dead by now. But there's the secret. A well-known secret. Officially, you are his daughter. The police are using you as bait to get him hooked; they've no evidence against him. Whoever turns informer is found the next day.

"What about the lounge? Don't they know about the lounge? Where so many orgies and crimes are committed? Every night, at least one corpse is smuggled out of there."

"They who know won't speak. It doesn't suit them to. Whoever went in there to investigate kept whatever he saw secret. He didn't tell anyone, because he never came out again live. Your Derry knows how to pay. He pays dear, but he wins..."

She stopped, A shadow swept over her face. Was it a fleeting sense of guilt?

"Why have you told me all this, Mammy? Aren't you afraid I'll let on?"

This time, she looked at me sadly.

"You won't, Terry. Because I know you hate your Derry as much as I hate him, and because you have no one else to turn to but me. Give me your hand and help me up."

I helped her to her feet. She put her hands round her middle.

"Oh," she said, "I've got such a pain. It must be my kidneys, sometimes, I can't bend down."

"You must go and see a doctor," I said, but she paid no attention to my words, as if she didn't heard my advice, then she went on.

"As long as I am alive, you've nothing to fear. I will look after you in my own way. Live your life, Terry. The life of a whore. Of a free whore."

"Since you hate Derry, do you kill for him?

"To live, my child, to live. I can't prostitute myself for hire any longer. No one will have me. And rather than be a beggar, I'm a murderess, and so, people respect me... Whereas beggars are not respected by anyone…"

"I'll pay you double what Derry pays you, Mammy, if you agree to kill for me."

She turned round and looked at me in amazement.

"To go against Derry? Are you mad? How can we stand up to him? We are two, and they are a hundred."

"We won't come out in the open. We'll kill on the quiet. Derry won't know. First of all, we must do in the old man who betrayed me and was the cause of the murder of Elena and of the shepherd. I want revenge, Mammy."

She went on looking at me. "I have heard say a lot about the Greeks, but now, I see for myself that the Greeks don't forgive injustice. I'll help you, Terry. But Derry has long ears and sharp eyes, so we must be very careful. We must let some time pass for the matter to blow over."

"Okay, Mammy, I'll tell you later who the next is to be."

She put on her heavy fur coat that make her look even bigger and funnier. And with her cigar in her mouth, she looked just what she was. A criminal drug addict.

"I must leave you now. I need my refreshment."

Her eyes were bright. She had to have her "charge". She banged the door shut. That showed how impatient she was. I lay down on my bed, but when I heard her car screech off, I sat up.

Advice from a whore like Mammy, I thought. *Advice..... Why not! Maybe she was right.* I stood in front of the mirror. I began to throw my clothes off one by one. I was beautiful.

The mirror confirmed Mammy's words. I had a pearly, well-formed figure, golden hair, like corn in the wind. Blue eyes and full, sensual lips. Lips made for kissing. I had heard from some of my lovers that the courtesans of Ancient Greece were very beautiful. And I was Greek…

Greek and beautiful! A young courtesan in the heart of New York. And from this day, I was going to start building my temple. Mammy was right. God has blessed love, so prostitution was blessed. Love was blessed. I was blessed. My body was on fire at that moment...

Naked as I was, I went down to the swimming pool. Derry had me brought to my own little villa.

I plunged into the water and felt fine. I had often seen well-dressed street walkers. I would be like them. *Why not?* I said to myself. I would wear silk undies next to my skin, smart, expensive dresses, I would sell myself to the rich... make money, lots of money. I would first look at their wallets and then at their faces. Before I got like Mammy. Before I was crossed off the official list of whores, I would be rich. It was the only way to protect myself.

From that day on, I sold my body with no discrimination. I flung myself whole-hardly into my new "business", and when I wasn't selling love or peddling dope, I was window-shopping and planning my new wardrobe, which was always of the latest fashion.

The bills mounted. I kept on needing more and more money. Derry no longer took anything from my purse. He was content with the money I got from pushing drugs. And it wasn't a little. Every day, I would give him over two thousand dollars. Business was good; it ran smoothly. As smoothly as our agreement. Our customers increased from day to day. The police didn't suspect me. I was clever at finding original ways of channeling the drugs and of collecting the money. Derry was delighted with me. So he didn't interfere with my private life.

I would not accept any share in the drug money. Now, I, myself, chose the customers I would sell myself to. I was only interested in their wallets. I got into the most posh hotels by various pretexts, and then, I would bring my female weapons into play and pick up my customers. Sometimes, I would sleep with a waiter or a barman to get the information I needed about the patrons of the hotel. They'd tell me in detail all I wanted to know.

The rich aristocrats who wanted to keep their family honor intact, but have a good time all the same, were the best payers. That's the way I preferred them. I had a notebook with a list of their names and the sum I could charge each one. The presents I received were fabulous: smart cars, fabulous jewels, which I chose and which they paid for. I could hardly meet the demand. I had a bank account that a well-paid film star would envy. All doors were open to me, I lived a grand life, and I had moved into a larger villa. I had servants, a chauffeur-driven car...

And yet I was only a child, Mr. District Attorney. A girl of seventeen...

My ambition was to become a tip-top prostitute. I had to be the best. I had to hold the scepter. So, I would employ people who could give me lessons on how to behave like a lady. But I couldn't put up with them for more than a day. I didn't know exactly what I wanted. At times, I thought I was lost. The bond that tied me to Derry was throttling me. I knew that the drugs I pushed were the cause of many deaths. But I could not stop. If I did, I would have to give up my free life as well. At those difficult times, Mammy was a source of strength until the day I could put my plan into practice. She bucked me up and told me to be patient.

My seventeen years were a heavy burden. Booze is a great invention, Mr. District Attorney. When my conscience started pricking me, I would resort to booze. In every room in my villa, there was a little bar well-stocked with expensive drinks of-all brands of poison. Public bars were not a patch on mine.

In drink, I forget my weariness and my worries. Derry's threats, my lost dreams. But I could never forget Elena. I could never forget the shepherd. Those two gave me the strength to carry on. They gave me courage to go on living my sinful life. I was waiting for the moment when I would crush my enemies.

"I'll crush them," I would say to Mammy. "I'll crush them."

As for my parents, I never even thought of them. How can you think of someone you have hardly ever known? My mother was unknown to me, by her premature death. My father's death was a release. My stepmother was often in my mind, and I could not wait to impose a worthy punishment on her.

What kept me alive was the dream of revenge, nothing else. I had turned into a little spider, weaving its web to catch those it hated. I thirsted for revenge...

In my world, in the underworld of lawlessness, there is a law. But I think this law applies in your lawful world, too, Mr. District Attorney (why on earth do you call yourselves lawful).

The law is MIGHT IS RIGHT. Am I wrong? No, please tell me, doesn't the big fish eat the little one?

Three years had passed since Elena and the shepherd had died. On the third anniversary of their death, I was making love with a famous general in a third-rate hotel, for more secrecy... he paid me well. But as he said, he didn't pay me for my body only, he wanted my soul, too. He wanted to keep me near him always. His plan was a military one. That is, I would serve him for as long as he needed me, and then he would give me my discharge. But that was not my idea. I had another plan in mind.

That's why I put up with him, and even granted him a discount on the usual price I had put on my body...

THE GENERAL AND I

I got out of bed and walked across the room, waddling my fanny provokingly. I passed in front of him, stark naked as I was, and went towards the mirror.

"You've got such a wonderful body," he said. He came near and began to paw me. He was a well-built man, dark and good-looking. Even naked, he looked every inch a general!

He always kept to his military strategy, even in bed with me. He would never make love more than once. That would be a waste of strength, he said.

"I know I've got a fine body." I said, as I stretched myself languorously, like a cat, I went and sat on the bed, swinging my legs to and fro. "But what's the good," I went on, "I'm nothing but a prostitute.

A super-prostitute, it's true. There are very few to hold the candle to me..... but nevertheless, I'm a prostitute. I've told you to stop saying you want to keep me near you, and stop treating me like a soldier under your command. No army regulations for me, thanks. The moment your back is turned, there will be someone else ready to take your place. I can't bear to be alone, besides, I'm very much in demand with wealthy old blokes, and in general with the rich...". I spat the chewing- gum out and curled up among the bed-clothes.

I had to carry out my plan quickly, because Mammy was waiting for me two blocks away in the hired car…

He came near me again, scratching his head.

"You've been with me for a week now, why did you do it?"

"I had to do my military service. To learn something about the army—to prepare a frontal attack. My aim is victory."

I like military strategy, but mind you, only in certain cases...

"He lay down next to me, laughing, and turned to take me in his arms. I laughed, too, but drew away. I recoiled like a cat, ready to spring, then, I turned and jumped out of bed.

"Spare your beautiful body, don't ruin it, by going with all kinds of men, my sweet Terry," he said, ogling me. ning my body! that's sLsiy, ruined, useless. Tomorrow, next day, in a few days} time, in.

"He, ha, ha! Talk about ruining my body! That's already ruined useless. Tomorrow, next day, in a few days' time, in a few years, my body will be a repulsive skeleton with torn bits of flesh hanging to it, food for the worms, like so many other beautiful bodies. Like Elena's body," I cried as I seized the bottle that was on the bedside table. I had to drink to ease the pain in my heart. Two tears ran from my eyes. I couldn't stop them.

"Terry, honey, why are you crying?" he asked in surprise.

"Never ask a whore why she's crying, she can't tell you. Just like a man that's been hanged - he never knows why he's left to dangle from the gallows long after his body is lifeless (and naturally harmless). A whore and a hanged man, it's the same thing. Dead-dead, both of them. People despise public whores but they respect aristocratic ones. They are worse than alley cats. You are a soldier. You are supposed to keep law and order, but at this very minute, you are violating the law, tumbling a whore who is still under-age, and you've got a wife and children.

But excuse me, I forgot that your stars on your uniform hide your true self."

"But I love you, Terry" he said, as he half-rose.

"Don't move from where you are, General. We are not in barracks now, and I'm not a soldier to take orders from you. Now, you'll listen to me. I'm going to give orders, and you're going to obey… I'm making a frontal attack, so you try to defend yourself honorably… For how long will you love me, General? Until you or I get new orders. You soldiers think you've got the world at your feet, as long as you are young, But when you are retired, you seek the love and the sympathy of those you formerly despised and looked at from on high. Shall I tell you something? You're not a good General."

"Why, Terry?"

"Because all these days we've been trying to use me as a screen to sell U.S.A. secrets to foreigners."

He went as yellow as a lemon. Then, he began to tremble.

"Don't tremble," I said "I don't care about such things. All I want you to do now is to have a drink with me. Why won't you drink?"

"Don't you really care about those documents?"

"Do what you like with them; I couldn't care less. I was never interested in politics. I am allergic to them. Those are things I can't understand. I can't bear. I've no intention of becoming a Mata Hari. My business is less dangerous, it gives me no headaches. I want you to drink just because you obey me. I'm giving orders now, you see."

"That's your only reason?"

"Yes, it is."

"If I drink, will you think I'm a good general?"

"The best."

"Okay, fill up my glass."

I went to the bathroom cupboard to get a glass. At the bottom of the glass was a white powder, which I'd put there previously. That was my aim: to drug him. To be free to act as I liked, to destroy the documents in his case, and to steal his gun.

Of course, I could have bought a gun. But I knew that Derry and his mob were keeping their eyes on me, and I didn't want them to get wind that I need a gun. Mammy, who was helping me carry out my plan of revenge had told me to be careful, very careful... She had provided me with a good dose of the white powder, from her personal supply.

And when I told her that a General wanted my company, she rubbed her hands with joy and told me to jump at the opportunity. Then, she advised me what to do... Mammy was a clever old harlot...

"Mind, Terry, no one must suspect that we need a gun. Of course, with a few dollars, I could get you a dozen guns, but don't forget that Derry and his gorillas are on the look-out, and the police, too... So, this general will pay a debt of honor for the use of your body... He won't guess anything. Do as I say."

So, I did what Mammy advised me to do. When the General was lying drugged on the bed, I got up and dressed hurriedly. I took the documents and the gun out of the case and put them in mine. Then, I put a "do not disturb" card on the door. I left the hotel by the back door, so as not to be seen by the hall porter. In a few minutes, I was in my car. A short while later, I was with Mammy in the hired car. I ran and sat next to her. She kissed me.

"Okay, Terry?"

"Okay, Mammy. But I've found out that the General is a traitor."

I told her about the documents I'd found in his care and that I'd now got in my own bag.

"Let me have a look at them," said Mammy. I gave them to her, and she examined them carefully. Then, she spat out of the car window.

"The bastard," she swore, "the lousy swine, I'll spit on his balls. He wants to stir up trouble in this country. We'll hand him over to the authorities, Terry."

"But how?" I asked.

"How? It's simple –just a phone call. The only thing is that you'll have to put those papers back into his case…

YOU MUST KNOW HOW TO KILL

Mammy and I got out of the car outside the old man's villa. She hid behind me, as I rang the bell.

"Who is it?" called the old man.

"I, Terry, honey."

He seemed taken aback. He hadn't seen me for three years. "Terry, little Terry."

"Yes, I."

"Alky, Alky," I heard him calling. "Open the door, it's Terry, our little Terry. I haven't seen her for three years. I'm so glad she's come."

Mammy looked at me with a broad smile and squeezed my hand.

"Now we've got them both," she muttered.

But I was scared. I hadn't expected Alky to be there. I thought the old man would be alone. Mammy sensed my fear.

"Don't be afraid," she said. "As long as I'm with you, you've nothing to fear. You leave this to me. The old man doesn't know I'm with you, but Alky does..."

She had hardly finished speaking when the door was opened. Alky was dressed up to the nines. That made me wonder still more.

Mammy had never told me that Alky would be there. Our agreement had been to kill them one by one. Twenty thousand dollars for both. Ten thousand each. Mammy was hard up, and she had to improve her finances and provide for her old age, as she used to say. Her expenses increased from day to day as she grew older and her flesh began to sag on her body.

The doses of dope increased, she needed more and more to satisfy her craving.

" So you've brought Terry, too," said Alky, as he put his hands in his pockets. "Why the hell have you brought that loose-tongued bitch along with you? "

"I thought that was in our agreement. Stop jabbering, and finish off the old man, hey presto..."

"The dough."

Mammy opened her handbag and took out a fat bunch of notes. His eyes were fixed on the money, and you could read cruelty and hate in them.

"Don't try any tricks on me," said Mammy. " You know you'll have to do with the boss if you even harm a hair of Terry's head."

"I know our boss adores his little daughter," said Alky, ironically. "But I'll finish off the old bastard, although I don't know what good his death will do us. He pays our girls well, and we all get our share."

"Stop gassing; you're wasting our time. You'll know the reason later. That rotten old blackguard must die."

At that moment, we saw the old man approaching with outstretched arms, "Terry, little Terry, welcome..."

His eyes turned upwards, and he fell without uttering a single word. He crumpled to the ground, and only for a moment did his eyes look upon my petrified face. But satisfaction must have been so evident there that he understood why he had to die. Alky had drawn the dagger out of the old man's back and was wiping it clean, on a towel. But when he lifted his gaze, he saw Mammy covering him with the general's gun. I stood looking on, all smiles.

"What's the idea?" he stammered, ready to pounce on us.

"Is this a joke?"

"This is no joke," said Mammy, through clenched teeth.

"One step, and I'll send you packing to hell, hand in hand with this dirty old lecher."

"But what have I done to you?'

"Terry will answer that one "

I spoke up. "I'll tell you why I want you dead, my dear Alky. I'll my will plant the bullets. For four years, I've watched you torture all those young girls, in the most horrible way, forcing them to deprave themselves."

"Those were your Derry's orders".

"Who is my Derry? Our boss? The cursed pimp? His turn will come, too, don't worry. I won't leave you without a boss in the other world. What you have to worry about, is that your business won't get on so well there... You've hastened your death by killing Elena. This old stiff lying here, told you about my meeting with the shepherd. Who killed the shepherd? Speak up!"

"I killed him," he said with swagger, "and I'll kill you and this old whore who has tricked me."

"We'll see about that. I don't know your customs here merice, but in my country, Greece, traitors and murderers pay dearly. That's why we don't have much trouble from them. Bump him off Mammy—aim all the bullets at his heart, all of them..."

"Don't, don't, don't. Please, Terry, tell her to hold it. I'll never harm anyone again, and I'll your Derry, if you want me to."

"How often have your victims begged you for mercy? Have you kept count? How many have died at your hands? Goodbye, sweetie-pie".

Mammy pressed the trigger. I saw him double in two, "Shall I finish him off, Terry? asked Mammy, drinking out of a bottle she held in her left hand.

"Yes, do, and mind you, all the bullets in his heart…"

She went near him and pushed him with her foot. She turned him over on his back, and began to fire. She only stopped when she heard the gun click.

"Put the gun back where it came from, and thank the General," she said giving me back the gun. " We must be polite to the gentlemen, Terry. It's a good gun, though. The General knows how to choose his weapons."

"Well he's a General, isn't he?"

"Of course, you're right. Anyway, we didn't need it for long.

Twenty minutes to get rid of those two snakes. The operation was successful. Go to the car, I'm coming..."

She soon joined me, and we drove off under the protection of darkness. We took the same way back. The general was still in a coma-like sleep. I put the gun back in its place, after wiping it clean of fingerprints. I put the tell-tale documents back into his case, and then I wrote on the mirror, with my lipstick, in capital letters: "GENERAL, YOU ARE A TRAITOR."

In the lobby, the hall-porter looked at me strangely.

"Are you leaving so soon?, Alone, why?"

"He's asleep", I said.

"I see," said the hall porter.

"You do, do you? I asked.

"Yes, that nothing..."

"Ah!" I said, "You're smart, aren't you?"

When I was in the street again, I did as Mammy had told me. I went to the first phone box and asked the operator to connect me with the offices of one of the military services.

When I was connected, I gave them the name and address of the hotel and the number of the room, where they would find the General and the documents.

I hung up without waiting to hear their answer... I was in a hurry to get to the nearest bar. I was thirsty. I wasn't interested in the General any longer...

The barman looked at me inquiringly, but he served me. From then on, that bar became my regular haunt.

We gradually got friendly, the barman and I. He would advise me not to drink, but his advice fell on deaf ears.

He knew nothing about two murders that had been committed within twenty minutes, in a luxury villa.

He knew nothing about my dear Elena, and the kind shepherd. He had not seen two pairs of eyes fixed on him. He hadn't said, "All the bullets in his heart." He wasn't haunted by Elena's last words, "So you, too, wanted to kill me, Terry."

He had not died young and come to life again in hell. He was not tortured, nor forced to kill by pushing dope. He didn't have to hire out his body. He wasn't a girl to have to carry out Derry's orders, he hadn't paid twenty thousand dollars to rid the world of two monsters in human form.

"Another double whisky... two double whiskies... come on, Boy... I wonder if the General has read the words on the mirror. Have they netted him? Or has he given them the slip?"

"What general?" he asked.

"One more drink, Boy, And don't get mixed up with generals. You'll land yourself in trouble. You see to your bottles. That's where your future lies. And take it from me, when there's money in your pocket, you can shit on everybody, even on generals. Let's have another one, Boy."

"What have you got against generals? "

"I once got involved with a general, and it did me no good."

His eyes were begging me to stop drinking, but I pretended not to understand.. "I want some more drink, Boy. I'm paying you, aren't I? So since I pay you, you've got to top up my glass as soon as it empties..."

"Don't you know what you're doing to yourself?"

"Cut the crap, Boy. I can't stomach preaching. I was born a whore, and raised as one, And if it were not for the likes of me, you'd soon shut down your bloody bar..."

Whenever there weren't many people in the bar, he would try to talk me into giving up the bottle.. "Your youth," he would argue.

"Yes, Boy, it's because of my youth that I'm drinking. Drink clouds my mind and makes me forget. To forget, that's why I'm drinking. I come here to spend my money in your bar because you're my friend."

ABOUT THE AUTHORS

TUYEN HOANG

My name is Tuyen Hoang. I was born in Vietnam. According to my mother, in 1980, my family was not a wealthy or lucky family like some other families. At 10 years old, I looked like I was just 6 years old because I didn't have milk to drink, nor much food to eat. Meat at that time was very expensive, so all we ate was white rice with corn and beans. While watching my friends have food to eat and milk to drink, I would go home and cry so much that my mother would make me milk from rice. As a child who never tasted cow's milk before, the rice water that my family considered "milk" is to this day my favorite drink in the world. Living in such a small town with no money, my dad had a plan to help us get out of this situation as he understood how difficult it was on me and my mom. Even when I didn't have a lot of opportunities, I still had a big dream. As an eight year old, I knew how to help my mom sell food to earn money. My mom always told me, "When things get hard, remember that there are a lot of people who have to go through rough times too. Everyone has their own paths, but that doesn't mean that we can just rely on that path without fighting. Success doesn't come if you don't try."

Now, I'm not the eight year old girl anymore. It has been 33 years. I am 41 with a lot of experiences. There were times when I failed; times when I was all alone. I didn't give up. I learned to stand up on my own and accomplish my dream. I was able to help other people. Now I realize that this is my purpose in life. I hope with my warm and motivating heart, I will be able to help more people in the future and to send them the message that an 8 year old me always remembered: "Don't alter your dream to fit your reality…Upgrade your conviction to match your destiny." I can do it and you can do it too.

MARIA TZIMAS

Maria Tzimas was born in war ravaged Greece, December 1942, in the small village of Preveza. She contracted polio at the age of three. This was the beginning of her personal and physical struggles and forty-seven operations.

All through this period she was enrolled in schools and her studies were sent to her bedside. She applied herself diligently and wrote profusely. At the age of 14, she wrote a small novel titled "FIGHTING WITH THE WAVES" and realized her first money for her talent. Commissions for special articles for local newspapers followed.

Surprisingly, at the age of 16, she wrote a book called "I ACCUSE YOU", which became an overnight bestseller throughout Greece in 1965. The book was based on her experiences in many hospitals, prompted many of the newspapers and magazines to write her true life story. Her illness still continued to torment her, yet prod her to greater effort at one time and the same time.

She continued her writing efforts while attending the University of Pantion, Studying Law. Her basic drive to write effected her switch to the school of reporting. Then fate struck. She met Mrs. Helen Vlahos, noted publisher of several daily newspapers, who retained her as a feature writer for the newspapers and magazines.

Her continuing crippled condition forced her to seek medical aid in the United States and, at the age of 21, after the final two operations at Midtown hospital, New York, she was able to walk with some greater freedom (without crutches) but still with a cane.

Love and marriage promoted her return to Greece. However the dictatorship prohibited the sale of any of her writings. The dubious distinction of being the only Greek author to receive a decree of Prohibition from the Greek Government forced her and her family back to the United States in the hope that her talent would find fulfillment there.

"YOUTH IN THE WIND" her latest work, reflects the majority gathered through the years. It is a reflection of the revolution of today's young people.

The human being is neither an angel nor a beast.
The great misfortune is the one who appears to be an angel
But is really a beast.

CHILDREN are like flowers.
Both are beautiful but lack strength.
Flowers die once, but children are maltreated every day.

The child, since the creation of the world, has been the victim of all the sadists and perverts, such Herod and Hitler, and so many others, who are daily responsible for numerous childhood tragedies. Then we shall see how the child has been victimized.

Many organizations have been formed to protect the children, but looking around us, it seems ironic that they are not able to do very much.

Pain does not have color, but it has a face and we see that face daily, in millions of pale and skinny faces.

Personally, I never was a child.
I never played with toys.
I never held a doll.
I lived a sad and melancholy childhood and I know its "cost"

YOUTH IN THE WIND, is a story that will touch everyones HEART,
and will give hope to a younger generation.

Maria Tzimas

CPSIA information can be obtained
at www.ICGtesting.com
Printed in the USA
LVHW050817290122
709581LV00003B/256